SCORPIONS
AND GILA MONST[ERS].
TOO DRY TO [GROW ANYTHING]
Americans had opened up an exotic territory
in the Southwest.

NOW THEY HAD TO FIGURE OUT
HOW TO LIVE THERE.
Three meals a day, but the only menu item is beans.
A pet dog goes crazy from the heat and commits
suicide. School children practice "Indian drills" —
escaping to a nearby mine tunnel in case of attack.
A man's skull is crushed — and there's no surgeon.

BUCKSKINS,
BEDBUGS & BACON

From the mundane to the painfully bizarre,
Territorial tidbits of real life out west
will tickle your fancy.

🔫 🔫 🔫 🔫 🔫

Read other books in the
WILD WEST COLLECTION,
fast-paced, real-life stories of when the Old West
was still young and rowdy, where anything
could happen — and too often did.

🔫 🔫 🔫 🔫 🔫

DAYS OF DESTINY
MANHUNTS & MASSACRES
THEY LEFT THEIR MARK
THE LAW OF THE GUN
TOMBSTONE CHRONICLES
STALWART WOMEN
INTO THE UNKNOWN
RATTLESNAKE BLUES

Turn to the back of this book to learn more about them.

Design: MARY WINKELMAN VELGOS
Production: BETH ANDERSON
Photographic enhancement: BETH ANDERSON
Front cover art: TRACY BRITT
Tooled leather design on covers: KEVIN KIBSEY AND RONDA JOHNSON
Book editor: EVELYN HOWELL

FRONT COVER ART:
This collage of historical photographs, designed and rendered by artist
Tracy Britt against the faded backdrop of a Phoenix farmer plowing near
Camelback Mountain, includes (clockwise from top left): an 1870 family
portrait; an execution notice; a desert mesa; an adobe ruin; a cowboy holding
a baby; a vintage lantern; wagon travelers on the Arizona Strip; negative
of a father and son posing with rifles; an 1883 portrait of a Chiricahua Apache
couple; and a buffalo soldier.

Published by the Book Division of *Arizona Highways*® magazine, a monthly
publication of the Arizona Department of Transportation, 2039 West Lewis
Avenue, Phoenix, Arizona 85009. Telephone: (602) 712-2200
Web site: www.arizonahighways.com

Publisher — Win Holden
Managing Editor — Bob Albano
Associate Editors — Evelyn Howell and PK Perkin McMahon
Art Director — Mary Winkelman Velgos
Production Director — Cindy Mackey

Printed in the United States
Library of Congress Catalog Number 2001086530
ISBN 1-893860-22-1

BUCKSKINS,
BEDBUGS & BACON

Daily Adventures in the Old West

by CHIPS MUEHL

To
Bill, Jody, and Tim Muehl

**TWO MEN WITH THEIR PACK HORSES,
OAK CREEK CANYON, ARIZONA TERRITORY, 1897.**

A C K N O W L E D G E M E N T S

I am indebted to several people: to Howard Lamar of Yale University for launching me on my inquiries into the 19th-century West; to Robin Glassman, who suggested the book idea; to my son, Jody, for stirring my interest in the Southwest; to my husband, Bill, who encouraged me from start to finish; and to Nancy Dearborn, for all her help.

**STOPPING FOR THE NIGHT,
THESE TRAVELERS REST BY THE CAMPFIRE.**

Chips Muehl may seem the ideal nom de plume for an author specializing in Western history, but Ruth D. Muehl never coined the name just to suit a future book cover. "Muehl" (pronounced MEEL) is her married name, and "Chips" has been her nickname ever since a memorable childhood game of poker. Everyone has called her Chips from that day to this.

Chips started life on the East Coast, born and raised in New Haven, Connecticut.

She recalls long being fascinated by the American West. It was wide-open country that represented a beckoning freedom to her. An avid mountain hiker from about age 13, Chips did spend two weeks on a Sierra Club hike in California when she was 15 and climbed Pike's Peak while in her twenties — a hike that she recalls started out at midnight.

Still, she says, she "comes from a bunch of New England fuddy-duddies. Nobody in *my* family ever moved out West."

In fact, she moved away from New Haven only while she was in college, first at Wellesley and then at the University of Michigan. Graduating with a political science degree (with a minor in history), she returned to New Haven to start her married life there.

Also earning a masters degree, Chips taught ancient and medieval history at a private school. She later taught English as part of an inner-city GED preparation program and at the University of New Haven.

She wrote articles on various topics for *American Heritage* and *Yale Alumni Magazine* and published poetry in *Appalachia*. History was still a driving interest, and the West still tickled away, so Chips started to focus her research on the lives of women who traveled the Oregon Trail.

Then, in the mid-1980s, one of their two sons introduced Chips and husband Bill to *Arizona Highways* magazine and the Southwest in general.

That was the catalyst for this particular New Englander's long-standing fascination. By the early 1990s, she and Bill had moved to Bisbee, Arizona.

Before long, she was submitting historical pieces to *Arizona Highways*. The seeds for this book grew from those first research forays into the sun-baked, blizzard-driven gypsy jumble of personal stories that Chips found in the annals of Arizona history.

After four years in Bisbee, the Muehls moved to Tucson, where they've lived for the past six years. They and their Yorkshire terrier winter in Arizona and summer in New Hampshire. They love visiting their two grandchildren, Michael and Hannah, and Chips, now 77, still treks the rugged White Mountains — the ones on the Atlantic Seaboard.

Having done some more hiking out West since those early treks, she admits that mountain ranges back East certainly don't challenge the Western ones for elevation. The trails, though are steep, rough, and demanding. A hiker's way is often strewn with boulders and ridged with large, gnarled tree roots.

She always did "really long hikes of about 27 miles." Does she still? Oh, yes, although many New Hampshire hiking buddies from the old days think she's something of a nut — they're content to stay home.

CONTENTS

SETTLERS RELIED ON THE PROTECTION OF THE ARMY'S
BUFFALO SOLDIERS AND INDIAN SCOUTS.

Against All Odds

T HE FRONTIERS OF THE OLD WEST, INCLUDING THE DESERT
outbacks of Arizona Territory, took a heavy toll on pio-
neering settlers. Failure and tragedy were familiar companions of these men and women, yet judging by the personal
accounts they left, many also experienced times of intense joy
and fulfillment.

"How little it takes to make men happy," artist Frederick
Remington mused as he gazed into the glow of a log fire one
night. A friend snored peacefully nearby. The setting was not
luxurious — a small mountain cabin with the wind howling
outside. At that moment, the famous artist of Western scenes
sensed that happiness on the 19th-century American frontier
could be ephemeral and still be the often palpable reality that
Territorial pioneers recalled in later years.

Contentment in the midst of nature, intense satisfaction
in meeting frontier challenges to life and limb, joy in community
with others on a landscape where people were few and far
between — James Tevis tasted this blend of emotions while
roughing it in the Arizona wilderness. In 1857, he was on a
September hunting expedition with Mose Carson near Aravaipa
Canyon. Each night after supper, they would bed down by
their campfire in the autumn darkness, and Carson, an old
guide and trapper who was also Kit Carson's brother, would
reminisce about his many adventures. "I don't think I ever enjoyed anything more in my life than that excursion," Tevis as-
serted years later.

J. Ross Browne found similar satisfactions while touring
Sonora, Mexico, and Arizona Territory. One of Mark Twain's
contemporaries, a newspaper journalist, and a popular author,
he wrote humorously toned travel articles about the Southwest
at a time when few newspaper readers had ever thought to

**A GLIMPSE OF SOLITUDE: TWO MEN CAMP
ALONG THE COLORADO RIVER, JANUARY 1899.**

venture there. Risk of Apache attacks was high, so Browne
traveled with a group of U.S. Army soldiers.

"It was a cheery sight," he wrote with tongue-in-cheek
disregard for the very real threat, "to see our little command of
soldiers seated around the glowing campfires . . . the fumes of
many a savory mess regaling the senses, while song and joke
passed merrily around . . . It was all easy holiday life, with just
adventure and danger enough to give it zest. I had some no-
tion of giving up civilization altogether."

Not everyone who came West stopped to analyze why
they stayed, even when common sense strongly suggested some
wiser course of action. Decades after Browne's adventures,
when the influx of miners, soldiers, and settlers supposedly
made the Territory much more "civilized," violent circumstance
challenged many a person's will to hang on.

Stagecoach driver Jack Keating faced such challenges for
years as he carried the mail by stage from Silver King and Pinal
to Florence. Silver King was an immensely rich mine, and many
times Keating had to hand over the strongbox to some gunman
eager for a quicker way to grasp the mine's wealth. He was
held up so many times that he developed a routine whenever he
saw a stranger approaching him on the road: "He would halt his
team, clasp the lines between his knees, and raise his hands

HISTORIAN, AUTHOR, TRAVELER, AND
STATEHOOD LOBBYIST SHARLOT HALL OF
PRESCOTT, ARIZONA TERRITORY, REVELED
IN HER FREEDOMS AS A FRONTIER WOMAN.

high over his head. If the stranger turned out not to be a bandit, Jack would wax indignant. 'All right,' he'd say, 'but by God, I'll bet th' next one of ye'll ask for the box!'"

The lonely landscape harbored violence of many kinds, but there were those who found a peace there that they could experience nowhere else. George Ruxton, traveling the Territory in the mid-1800s, felt most contented when alone with just his horse and mules and the "attendant coyote which nightly serenaded us. I would sit crossed-legged enjoying the genial warmth and, pipe in mouth, watch the blue smoke as it curled up."

Army wives of the day, like Luna Willard and Josephine Clifford, who followed their soldier husbands to some of the harshest outposts, cherished the memory of an unexpected exhilaration always missing before. Luna exulted in a "keen sense of freedom" when she rode horseback near Camp Verde. Journeying from Tucson south to Tubac, Josephine Clifford relaxed at the end of a long day with evening rides among the wildflowers and watched "sunsets with their brilliant but delicate hues such as I have never seen elsewhere," at such times feeling "a sense of unbounded joy and freedom."

Martha Summerhayes, famous for her frontier memoirs of life as a soldier's wife, refused to let frequent frail health dim her enjoyment of simple pleasures: "Surely it is good to be in the army, I then thought; and after a supper consisting of soldiers' hot biscuit, antelope steak broiled over the coals, and a large cup of coffee, I went to rest [in her tent], listening to the soughing of the pines."

Sue Sumers came to Florence from San Francisco in 1879. "How free from care everyone seemed to be," she said, noting that dancing was the greatest pleasure for her neighbors. Impromptu social affairs were often assembled "and the slogan would be, 'On with the dance. Let joy be unconfined.'"

Wholehearted pleasure in each other's company sustained many through otherwise impossible situations. Jennie Parks Ringgold was one of two girls and five boys living on a Burro Mountains ranch: "We were a very happy and congenial bunch, creating most of our good times. We were cheerful and lively and very fond of each other, and we found many incidents irresistibly funny."

Good times or bad, frontier folk knew the value of the hopeful gesture and worked not to forget life's celebrations, big or small. A child in a Mormon company on the Mogollon Rim, Frank Pomeroy recalled Christmas 1846: "A few bold voices shouted Christmas greetings from wagon to wagon as the heads peered out from the covers and tents of the company." A heavy snowstorm forced them to abandon any thought of a more vigorous observance, and the group struggled to cover just a few miles that day. Another settler's boyhood Christmas remained a somber memory of "bedbugs, sickness, blizzards, lack of medical care, and death," yet more often, people recalled holidays made special by a heightened sense of community and the satisfaction of improvising everything from musical instruments and recitations to presents, decorations, and tree ornaments.

FREEDOM FROM CARE DIDN'T MEAN FREEDOM FROM DOING LAUNDRY. BISBEE, ARIZONA TERRITORY, 1885.

For settlers like the industrious Mormons, happiness could be drawn from the work itself. As he thought about the effort of building his house and others in the northern Arizona town of Snowflake in 1879, Joseph Fish wrote in his autobiography: "A person sometimes takes as much pleasure in building a home as in occupying it after it is built. The life of a pioneer is a hard one, but it is mingled with rays of light and joy in seeing waste places made to blossom."

E.R. Dewitt, who lived in Greer, said: "We all farmed, had cattle and sheep and made butter and cheese, worked for wages, freighted, run in debt but always paid; fished and hunted and were always happy and never paid a license."

Circumstance was all in how you saw it. Around 1840, George Ruxton was sloshing through a night of torrential rain when he saw an old man sitting on the ground. "His features pinched with the cold . . . his hunting shirt hanging about him in a flabby and soaking embrace . . . Not for one instant intending it as a satire," the old man gustily sang: "How happy am I — From care I'm free — Oh, why are not all — Contented like me?"

Tucking In
and Tuckered Out

Keeping body and soul together —
with a little food, some water, a modest shelter —
was a task that sometimes a beleaguered pioneer
was just too hot and tired and bug-bitten to manage.

———◆———

Beans for breakfast
Beans for lunch
And beans for dinner too —
Anyone would really think
That once a day would do.

THIS BIT OF NEW ENGLAND DOGGEREL MIGHT HAVE BEEN written to describe the diet of most early comers to the Southwest. Not just solitary prospectors carrying their food in saddle bags but even hotels in the 1860s leaned heavily on beans, supplemented by beef, mutton, or venison. In Prescott's Juniper House, the only vegetable or fruit item that appeared on their July Fourth 1864 menu was apple roll.

Most, like preacher Charles Gillett of the Verde Valley Mission, had little choice. The preacher farmed and freighted goods to support his family. On freighting expeditions, meals consisted of "bacon and bread, or flapjacks — flour mixed with water and fried in bacon grease." He recalled, "I have seen my dog actually refuse to eat the same bread that I ate."

In 1870, Dr. Edward Palmer, traveling out of Fort Mohave along the bottom of the Colorado River, arrived hungry and thirsty at the primitive hovel of two nearly naked white men. Invited to

**EATING OUTSIDE A CANVAS-SIDED
CHUCK WAGON, CIRCA 1900.**

stay for supper, Palmer was confronted by "some boiled lean beef, blue and nearly without taste," unpalatable yellow bread, and dirty black molasses. Able to eat but a few mouthfuls, the doctor was faced the next morning with more of the same for breakfast. "I paid my bill," he recalled, "and left with pleasure."

Still, liquor and a sense of humor could help miners swallow their barely edible fare after a hard day's work underground. With this thought in mind, no doubt, the proprietor of a little restaurant near the Silver King mine posted a sign: Square Meal — 50 cents, Tuckout — 75 cents, Mortal Gorge — $1.

Army food for enlisted men also was nothing to sign up for. Sgt. Henry Yohn at Fort Lowell in 1866 remembered, "We had no fruit except pomegranites [sic] and limes from the South.

Never saw an egg in two years, nor tomatoes, had potatoes that were a greenish color inside at 40 cents a pound. We ate frijoles, tortillas. Principal diet was beans. We had no bacon — only salt meat from the East." Yet, fortified with a new cook and provisions, one Army officer and his men, traveling southeast from Tucson in 1872, enjoyed a supper of beefsteak with oysters, coffee, tea, bread and butter, and tomatoes.

Surprisingly, oysters of various kinds appear in many accounts. Canned cove oysters became tasty, according to Army wife Alice Baldwin, with the addition of eggs and cracker crumbs. At Fort Whipple, an officer once paid $7 for a dozen oysters shipped in cracked ice from Baltimore.

Even ranches did not customarily include a vegetable garden or a dairy herd. One notable exception was the Hooker ranch where the table was stocked with all kinds of vegetables, a dairy herd supplied fresh milk and butter, and hundreds of chickens and turkeys ensured eggs and poultry for the table. As early as 1857, Charles Poston in Tubac, aided by a German gardener, "soon produced all vegetables, melons, etc. that we required."

At the Shoo-Fly restaurant in Tucson in the 1860s and 1870s, the fare depended on current relations with the Apaches. When pack trains from Sonora, Mexico, could get through Apache territory safely, "the mutton, bacon, and egg menu was supplemented with oranges, apricots, lemons and quinces, lettuce and tomatoes." Occasionally, strawberries and figs appeared, and in 1869, the first ice cream was sold in Tucson.

Ingenuity was often responsible for gourmet touches. Alice Baldwin's Army cook, Bowers, unexpectedly produced a bottle of plum wine at a social gathering in camp en route to Fort Wingate, New Mexico. Bowers had made the wine from wild plums he gathered, cooked with sugar, and strained through a sock.

Bowers obviously knew that, in a time of few pleasant distractions and non-existent luxury, well-cooked meals could make the pioneer's life bearable.

Often denied other jobs because of their race, many Chinese immigrants worked as cooks in the Southwest. In the kitchen, they were known to produce gastronomic miracles under primitive conditions.

Army wife Ellen Biddle was entertaining a general at Fort Whipple. While all had gone smoothly, she had a moment of panic when her Chinese cook presented her with the evening's dessert course, which truly resembled a large fish. To her relief, the dish turned out to be a masterful work of edible sculpture — a perfect charlotte russe molded in the shape of a fish.

Not every Chinese cook was a model of perfection in all things. There was Judge Richard Sloan's intractable cook, Ing, who worked for him in Phoenix during the 1880s. Sloan was going on a trip, so he arranged for Ing to cook for his neighbor, John Ross. Later, Ross told Sloan how things went:

> The first morning . . . I found that Ing had cooked but one egg. I said to him, "Ing, I like two eggs for breakfast. Tomorrow morning, serve me with two eggs." The next morning I found but one egg. I again told him that I wanted two eggs for breakfast and to serve me with that number every morning thereafter. The following morning I found but one egg awaiting me. I then spoke to him sharply and told him that I must have two eggs for breakfast. The old Chinaman looked at me and said, "One egg plenty 'nuff for any man. Judge Sloan, he only eat him one egg for breakfast." In spite of all I could say, Ing quit then and there and returned to your house.

Cooks often had to work under extraordinarily rough conditions. In 1880s Bisbee, Manuel Simas, a Portuguese immigrant, and his Mexican wife had no building for their restaurant, but they didn't let that stop them. They set up shop under a large tree, where dust and high wind made the whole experience almost intolerable for cook and customer alike.

During roundup time on a ranch, "the cook had to be astir long before daybreak and have a hardy breakfast ready by the time it was light enough for the men to see to eat," one

**A CHINESE COOK WORKING
AT A YUMA-AREA MINE, CIRCA 1890.**

old-timer remembered. When the Army was on the move, the cook's call sounded at 4 A.M.

Good cooks knew their value. Some cooks even came armed for attacks on their dignity, like the cooks at the Pandora Ranch near Oracle. Edith Stratton Kitt grew up there in the 1880s: "The cooks in their flour aprons were, as a rule, big men or women with big reputations — and I have known them to carry knives in their belts to instill proper respect and keep the teasing, hungry cowboys from trespassing on their domain."

**A COWBOY EATS ON THE RANGE SOMEWHERE IN COCHISE
OR SANTA CRUZ COUNTY, ARIZONA TERRITORY, 1906.**

A drifting cowboy with nowhere to call home was unlikely to kick a gift horse in the mouth, especially if cakes or pies were part of the deal. Jack Webb, a bachelor rancher in Yavapai County, cooked for homeless cowboys needing somewhere to hole up. His place was a natural choice, since it literally was a hole — a cave built into the hill with railroad ties at the front.

One cowhand recalled turning up at Webb's place one day when the rancher had baked an "egg cake," a confection "about as heavy as lead and, in texture, about as dense."

With a straight face, Webb said, "This isn't a very good cake. I didn't have eggs enough. It takes 64 eggs to make a good egg cake; the hens are sort of falling off, and I only had 36."

Still, an unlucky cook might find a gun aimed at him. When police officer Charley Hood impatiently demanded faster service on his order of ham and eggs at Tucson's Saddle Rock Restaurant, the cook dared to express his resentment. Taking offense, Hood drew his .45 and began shooting. Some restaurant patrons made for the exit, while the chef applied himself to finishing the ham and eggs posthaste.

Hood was hauled into court later and fined $10.

In fairness, customers were more likely to respond to bad food or poor service with a laugh than with a gun. Charlie

**THIS OLD RANCH HAND
SITS FOR A QUICK BITE.**

Alzamora presided over the kitchen at the rear of Congress
Hall, a Tucson gambling establishment. A better gambler than
a cook, Charlie, "in the midst of frying some eggs, would rush
from the stove, smoking pan in hand, to lay a bet on the turn of
a card in the main saloon." Amused patrons took to calling him
"Frying Pan Charlie."

One hungry customer was less amused when, believing
Charlie's plea that he was out of food to cook for breakfast,
lent him money to buy provisions. After a long wait, the customer discovered that Charlie had spent his money gambling.

BUILT OF ADOBE, R. MASON'S WESTERN HOTEL IN
CONTENTION, ARIZONA TERRITORY, ALSO OFFERED MEALS.

As the early mining camps of mostly bachelors evolved
into communities with women and children, meals became
something more than the basic offerings of boarding houses
and hotels.

By the 1870s in Flagstaff, long-time resident and author
Platt Cline wrote, breakfast was an important meal, including
meat and eggs, flapjacks, homemade bread and butter, homemade jams and jellies, tea or coffee, and milk. At noon, the
major meal of the day usually included meat — mutton, beef,
pork, or wild game — potatoes, sometimes another vegetable
or two, home-canned fruit, and pie or cake. Supper was a lighter
meal but substantial.

In August 1888, Sadie Martin, a young bride of less than
a year, left Iowa to join her husband in Arizona. Even in the
extreme heat and sun, she learned there were ways to keep
food and drink cool: "It was so good to have the sun go down
and to take a long cool drink of delicious water from the great
Mexican *olla* — a porous clay vessel, which was kept cool by a
covering of wet gunny sacks. . . . I was soon to find that we
could keep our milk and butter cool and sweet by wrapping
damp cloths around the receptacles that held them and setting

them in the air. And as we were everlastingly thirsty, it was a relief to find there would be no dearth of cooling drinks."

Keeping meat from spoiling was almost impossible on the desert ranches, Sadie remembered. "A neighbor had killed a beef and sent word . . . we were all anticipating the great treat, as fresh meat was scarce on the desert. We cooked some delicious, tender steak for our evening meal and set the table outside, as was our custom [because of the heat]. Just as we were ready to sit down, someone shouted, 'Sand storm!'"

The family tried to cover the food with dish towels and aprons and carry it inside, but the wind blew the covers off: "The food was coated with sand in a second, and we could not eat a bite of it."

In the 1880s, the railroads brought in a welcome diversity of foods. The Headquarters Saloon in Socorro, New Mexico, offered "Swiss cheese, limburger, handkase, Holland herring, pigs' feet, tongue, and rye bread."

Hotels in many towns were offering an astonishing range of delectables by the 1890s. Flagstaff's Weatherford Hotel, for example, served all kinds of meat, East Coast oysters, ocean and stream fish, chicken and turkey, and a variety of desserts, including pies and cakes. In Tucson, the Cosmopolitan Hotel's menus included delicacies like turtle and oyster soups and desserts such as charlotte russe and blanc mange.

Still in those days of big appetites from hard work or travel by foot or horseback over rough terrain, an elemental meal might be the one enjoyed the most.

Rancher John Rockfellow wrote of a trip in the 1870s when he and his group reached the Bosque Ranch on the Santa Cruz River. As they sat down for supper, a crazy-looking, disheveled man stumbled into camp, speaking disjointedly.

Revived with a little supper, the man said he was George Atkinson and he had been held up six men. They took everything he had — mule, rifle, money, new Stetson hat, and boots. As a parting shot, one desperado had kicked him in the belly and sent him on his way.

AN APACHE WOMAN LAYS OUT SKINS TO CURE IN FRONT OF HER BRUSH SHELTER. WHEN THEY NEEDED READY SHADE, SETTLERS COPIED THESE HANDY STRUCTURES .

Years later when Atkinson — who had become a wealthy cattleman — and Rockfellow met in Tucson, Atkinson happily recalled, "Do you know, I never in all my years tasted anything so good as those beans and bacon we ate that night on the Bosque."

For soldiers of the U.S. Army, no posting was as unpopular as Arizona. Intense heat and extreme cold; rocky, confusing, cactus-studded terrain; vast expanses with no water — Arizona promised more hazards than most cared to voluntarily endure.

Anson Mills, a captain of the 3rd Cavalry, remembered leaving Arizona on a steamboat from Yuma: "We took off our shoes and beat the dust of Arizona over the rail, at the same time cursing the land."

An Army wife leaving after four years, exulted, "Ordered out at last! I felt like jumping up onto the table, climbing onto the roof, dancing and singing and shouting for joy."

Civilian life was certainly no easier. The chief occupations of mining and cowherding offered long hours and little profit for difficult, often dangerous work under the constantly lurking threat of attack. Until women arrived in any numbers, creature comforts were almost non-existent.

**BOARDERS LINE THE PORCH AT THIS MINING-TOWN
BOARDING HOUSE, CIRCA 1890.**

Yet from early times going back beyond the first Spanish explorers to the Territory's native peoples, a tradition had grown up that eased the misery of trekking the Southwest: generous hospitality extended to all who happened by.

"Hospitality is a savage virtue and disappears with civilization," said Charles Poston, a standout host in 1850s Tubac who made his home basically a "free hotel." From the earliest days to the start of the 1900s, strangers could generally expect a warm welcome in rural areas throughout Arizona Territory.

Poston said he always had company in those days, but no one was ever charged anything for "entertainment, horse-shoeing, and fresh supplies for the road." Indeed, if Poston had had a few more such guests, they would have "boarded him out of his boots," said J. Ross Browne, a travel writer who marveled at Poston's generosity in the face of high-priced provisions and scarce money.

As rough as it was readily given was the hospitality in towns like Tucson in the 1860s, according to Army sergeant Henry Yohn. "If you were invited," he recalled, "you slept with the whole family on a rawhide on the floor. Guests would always bring their own rawhides with them to sleep on."

Noted for the quality of their hospitality were well-to-do ranchers like Henry Hooker and John Slaughter. It was said that Hooker welcomed almost every prominent officer serving in southern Arizona between 1875 and 1900, along the likes of John Muir, Frederick Remington, and even Wyatt Earp and Doc Holliday after the shooting near the O.K. Corral.

Hooker asked little of his guests except that every man wear a jacket to dinner, even if he had to borrow one. But while payment wasn't asked, simple appreciation was an unwritten rule. One guest was treated with full hospitality, even though he had given Hooker peremptory orders about the care of his horse and had demanded a particular menu for dinner. The next morning, this guest made the mistake of asking for his bill.

"Twenty dollars," Hooker responded. The guest said, "That's pretty steep, isn't it?" "Yes, but that's my price," Hooker said. The man handed over a $20 bill. Hooker tore it into small pieces and threw it away, saying, "Now, get out of here and never let me see your face around my ranch again."

John Slaughter enjoyed company at his San Bernadino ranch in southeastern Arizona. It was said that if he was sitting on his porch when a stranger rode up, he would rise and ask him to have dinner and stay a spell. Like Hooker, Slaughter insisted that the men wear coats to dinner at the great dining room table that seated 25.

At King Woolsey's ranch in the 1860s, distinctions were made at table settings according to ethnic background and class. Mexican herders sat separately from Anglo workmen, who sat apart from the Woolsey family. Visitors were similarly separated, although everyone who turned up was welcomed. Judge Joseph Pratt Allyn noted that the table had been set 16 times in one day to keep up this custom, a surprising one on the otherwise fairly democratic frontier. When Allyn visited the Sheldon ranch near Fort Whipple in 1864, the table had to be reset four times, but solely because of over-crowding. Allyn had arrived with the Territorial governor's party en route to establishing the new Territorial capital, only to find another group of travelers already at the ranch. Sheldon welcomed them all and fed them huge stacks of venison and bread, gratis.

In those early days, people might even be free to make themselves at home when the owner of an establishment was away. Washing the dishes and leaving wood for the next fire were the only demands made on the visitor, according to Dr. Corbusier, an Army surgeon in the 1870s.

Another surgeon, Ralph Palmer, who worked at the Roosevelt Dam around 1904, remembered arriving at Jake Stauffer's cabin in a blizzard on his way back from a 65-mile trip to attend a sick woman. Within a short time five other men had joined Ralph and his companion, knowing that "Jake's cabin was always open for shelter." Mrs. Stauffer fed family and guests beans with salt pork, biscuits, honey, and coffee. Then all were bedded down in comparative comfort thanks to a plentiful supply of the Stauffer blankets.

The hospitality of women like Mrs. Stauffer was legendary. William Fourr recalled that Mary Woolsey, King Woolsey's wife, used to struggle out of bed at midnight at their ranch to cook for whatever men had been out "chasing Indians."

Frank Gyberg, working as a teenaged cowboy in Yavapai County, never forgot how Pearl Plummer, of the Plummer ranch, "rolled out and fixed something for stray men to eat," no matter what time of night they turned up. As he said in a tribute that could apply to all the generous men and women who extended themselves for strangers in Territorial days, "God bless her generous heart, we've lost the pattern and don't have many of that kind any more."

Ella Haigler arrived exhausted and low on funds at Camp Verde with a sick husband and seven children, the youngest being just three months. One old man, Henry Williams, offered

UNDERGROUND SANITATION RULES ARE STRICTLY ENFORCED. THIS TYPE OF CAR COULD BE CALLED A MINER'S "CHIC SALE" WOMEN WERE SELDOM WELCOME IN ANY MINE TUNNELS, SO NATURALLY THESE CARS WERE "FOR MEN ONLY."

**THE TOILET CAR — WHERE JEROME
MINERS ANSWERED THE CALL OF NATURE.**

to put up the whole family at his ranch until they could find a suitable place to live, one of countless acts of kindness from strangers that helped to define the American frontier.

Without the all-important "savage virtue," then — as Judge Allyn observed of Tucson in the 1860s — "this would be a sorry place for a stranger."

"There is no tavern or other accommodation here for travelers, and I was obliged to roll myself in my blanket and sleep either in the street or in the corale . . . the corale is where they keep their horses and mules, but I slept very comfortably as the ground was made soft by manure," traveler Phocion R. Way noted of his Tucson experience. He'd left Cincinnati for Tucson in 1858, and Arizona lodgings at that time were as laughably lacking as some were luxurious just 30 years later.

In 1864, a blacksmith said to a visiting friend, at bedtime, "Let's go home and turn in," and escorted his guest to the town plaza. There he proceeded to undress. The astonished companion asked, "What are you doing?" The blacksmith replied, "This is where I gen'rally sleep."

During this era a surveying party tried in vain to find lodging in the Prescott House, Prescott's one hotel, but this establishment provided only food, not beds. A local joked, "You can get beds in the Hotel de Hay Mow or the Place de la Corale."

John Spring stayed in an 1868 hotel where he complained that "the room, furnished with a cot, two blankets, a pillow stuffed with hay, a chair and a tin basin was reckoned at a dollar a day, or rather a night, as you were expected to clear out by eight o'clock on the following morning."

Bedtime misery came in many forms. Spring was traveling with a group in southern Arizona. One night they bedded down in an old ruined house at the foot of the Huachuca Mountains. "We had hardly lain down when we seemed to be alive with vermin, mostly fleas — fleas in squads, platoons, companies, battalions, regiments, brigades, divisions and the whole army corps!"

In addition, scorpions and centipedes, drawn from chinks in the wall by the fire's heat, overran the travelers. An army of mosquitoes followed — "they never missed a shot, each one accompanied by a buzzing not unlike that made by a distant shell traversing the air." Abandoning all thought of sleep, Spring and his friends saddled up quickly and left.

Spring suffered other sleepless nights in the desert. Lost en route to Fort Grant, he decided to catch some sleep until daybreak. Having tethered his horse to a palo verde tree, he lay down under another tree's overhanging branches to sleep.

"Immediately I made a masterful jump, as if bitten by a million tarantulas." He had picked a silvery yucca tree, which had shed crops of needles. By the next day, when poor Spring finally staggered into Tucson, he was running a high fever and faced the excruciating pain of having the yucca needles extracted one by one.

As late as 1880, the weary Arizona traveler might have been better off sleeping in the corral than in one of the newly erected hostelries in Tucson. Will Barnes, en route to a job at Fort Grant, stopped at the Cosmopolitan Hotel. The small room he was assigned turned out to have a dozen fully dressed occupants "in various grades of intoxication." Worse for him was the washroom with a long sink whose "reeking waste water" drained off into a pipe that led to the street.

Decent quarters for women were in even shorter supply, although an occasional gallant might help ease the discomfort of a traveling lady . Such was the good fortune of Bertha White, an 18-year-old school teacher who stopped at a small inn at New River in 1887. The establishment boasted only one sleeping room, so the innkeeper turned over his room for Bertha's sole use and posted himself outside the door for protection.

But progress was only a few years away, and by 1901, even a number of luxurious hotels had been erected. In Oracle, the Mountain View Hotel with 12 large rooms, featuring hot and cold running water, was owned and managed by William and Annie Neal, a black couple. Old-timer E.O. Stratton said this establishment "added greatly to the popularity of Oracle as a health and tourist resort."

Willcox boasted the Willcox House, with "fine food and excellent accommodations" and patent water closets and bathrooms added in 1900. As at other quality inns of the day, a dress code required that evening clothes or "Sunday clothes" be worn in the dining room. Most imposing was Jerome's immense Montana Hotel — 200 bedrooms and a main dining room that seated 400 — with "its pediments, heavy rails, and balusters, architraves and cornices."

PLUCKING CHICKENS AT THE RANCH.

Like many early travelers, one reporter had made a determined effort for several nights to catch a few winks. After a spate of wretched nights spent in a jerry-built structure where he could hear all the whispered secrets and gossips of his neighbors, this man dryly observed, "Good men and women are leaving this city every day simply because they are sleepy."

As early as 1857 the "Tucson bed" was famous throughout the Southwest, according to one historian. The traveler made this bed simply by lying on his stomach and covering that with his back.

In the Southwest, obstacles to a good night's sleep were legion, including extreme temperatures, battles with armies of

**A WOMAN AND GIRL DRAW WATER
OUTSIDE AN ADOBE RANCH HOUSE.**

insects, wild animals, hostile plant life, and sandstorms. Indians might watch with amusement the "ill humor of newcomers frantically hustling about trying to find a place to sleep," but for the Anglo, the fight for sleep was no joke.

In La Paz on the Colorado River in July 1864, Judge Allyn remarked on the nocturnal dangers of "stepping onto some tossing, sleepless, sweating sleeper on the sidewalk" of the main street. And Lieutenant Sweeney became ill near Camp Yuma in heat "too excessive to admit of sleep." His appetite failed, and he was "tormented with an unquenchable thirst."

At the other extreme, cold could prove fatal. Caught in a snowstorm in late March 1872, one Army officer spoke of how his men had to sit up by the fires all night to keep from freezing. In the morning it was a long time before he himself could thaw out his shoes enough to put them on.

No matter where Army wife Martha Summerhayes tried to sleep, she seemed to run into trouble. In an effort to escape the heat of their house in Ehrenberg on the Colorado River, Martha and her husband would lie down in the courtyard. More

THE QUARTERS AT EHRENBERG, WHERE THE SUMMERHAYES STAYED IN 1875, ON THE WESTERN EDGE OF ARIZONA TERRITORY.

than once, they were driven indoors by violent, suffocating sandstorms that materialized suddenly, leaving a layer of sand over everything.

On one Arizona trip , the Summerhayes stayed at a ranch where wildcats kept them awake by yowling as they leapt in and out of window openings. The cats set the dogs to barking, which started the babies crying. Sleep was over for that night.

At Fort Lowell in Tucson, Martha was still having sleep troubles of the four-legged variety. "One night I was awakened by a tremendous snort right over my face. I opened my eyes and looked into the wild eyes of a big black bull. I think I must have screamed, for the bull ran clattering off the piazza . . ."

Describing 1880 Tucson, one old-timer wrote: "And dogs. They were countless — big ones and little ones, hairy ones and hairless ones, scrubs and blueboods. They barked all night long, and when not barking, they were raising an equal level of sound by their fights."

Nobody suffered more from the tortures of a sleepless night than travelers on stagecoaches. Jammed in with no space to relax, passengers might drop off to sleep from sheer exhaustion.

"They simply passed out from days of tremendous . . . jolting," said Englishman William Tallack. Speaking of travel on night coaches in the 1850s, Dr. Joseph Tucker recalled, "You never encroached upon your neighbor, but upon waking you seldom failed to find him lying across you or snoring an apology in your ear." Awake again after what he thought had been hours of sleep, Tucker would find that only a few minutes had passed and that the jolting journey still stretched before them.

Traveling from Missouri in 1857, Raphael Pumpelly was warned to stay awake for the passengers' protection, to which end "my neighbors beat a constant tattoo with their elbows on my ribs." Delirious after a trip from the Rio Grande to Tucson, he remembered nothing until he was awakened by a pistol shot. Pumpelly had staggered off the stagecoach, entered a building, thrown himself on the floor of the first room he came to, slept 12 hours, and finally awakened "fully restored both in mind and body" — in the middle of a gaming room full of quarreling people.

Sleep deprivation proved more than one poor stage traveler could endure. He became seriously deranged, and the other passengers were forced to tie him down and leave him at the next station.

A day's travel in Arizona Territory was a distance generally set by the distance between watering holes, writer J. Ross Browne recalled of his Arizona trek in the mid-1800s. Much of the life-and-death drama of the day had as much to do with finding good water in a stricken desert as it did with encountering bullets and bandits.

But calling it water didn't necessarily make it readily drinkable — "You had to bite it off," one traveler said of the rank water he had to drink.

Maddeningly, travelers frequently came upon a water hole only to find that the contents were fouled by anything from salt to decomposing bodies — animal and human. People who drank there took their chances with illness and death.

Mormons going from Snowflake to Fort Apache in July 1879 found the water in one riverbed too salty to drink and, further on, smelling too strongly of dead fish.

**A SOLDIER FILLS A BUCKET AND CANTEEN
FROM A TINY WATER HOLE.**

In 1863, Charles Genung reached Indian Wells and found that the only water there was thickly covered with insects. Before he could drink any of it, he had to strain it through a handkerchief.

Going to the Verde Valley in 1877, the Bristow family stopped at a water hole and were waiting for the mud to settle before scooping up clear water to drink. One young fellow couldn't wait and took it in his head to wash his feet first. "We dipped no more water from the hole, and we hazzard him good and plenty," one member recalled.

Another day, the mules refused to drink because they smelled a man's bloody clothing in the water. The Bristow party found a corpse partially buried nearby.

James Bristow, a teenager while on this trip, remembered how his grandmother made the most of any water they had. Once, after washing laundry in a tub, she noticed that the water looked fairly clean, so she gave each grandson a bath in it. Since the precious water still looked too good to dump out, she then washed the dishes.

When water gave out completely, people resorted to truly desparate measures. The Bristow party tried to alleviate the dryness by putting pebbles in their mouths, but on an 1850s trip, John Reid had only the powers of his own persuasion. Reid

THESE MEN ARE PACKING WATER ON MULES
TO FORT VERDE, ARIZONA TERRITORY.

was traveling through southern Arizona with a friend named
Radford. Their water had run out some time before, but the
two men plugged on in hopes of finding a water hole. Radford
was so far gone that Reid recalled "his face was shrunken, his
eyes unusually hollow, his tongue swelled, and his lips parched."
Radford declare he could not go on and must die where he lay.

Reid told his friend sternly that he had been sorely mistaken about him, that he had thought Radford to be "brave and
altogether resolute, but that [now] he was about to show himself unreliable." Prodding Radford in a determined effort to save
their lives, Reid told him to get up and go at once to spring that
he described as gushing in just the next hollow. The description
was a lie, since Reid had no idea how far away the next water
was, but Radford stirred himself, and they both kept slowly on
until evening. They slept for a few hours and then started walking again. Only a short time later they indeed came upon a spring.

One group and its mules, en route to California from New
Mexico, were suffering from extreme thirst when they came
at last within a half mile of the Gila River. Pricking up her ears,
one mule "gave one long bray and struck a bee line for the Gila,
directly through the thick chaparral . . . away we went like the
wind to the banks of the Gila, into which she plunged her head

and never raised it till her sides were distended like a hogshead." The other mules and horses followed just as impetuously. Some of their riders were left hanging in tree branches or thrown to the ground or pitched into the river as the animals rushed to quench their thirst.

Dogs were companions, helpers, even life-savers. They would tackle any creature from bear to rattlesnake and take on any job from controlling wild cattle to scaring off hostile Apaches. But even an animal's keen senses eventually succumbed to heat and thirst. Major Worth of the United States Army was traveling with his company near desolate Beale Springs in 1857 when his red setter, Pete, unable to stand the alien desert any longer, "committed suicide" by heading for the mountains, never to be seen again. This behavior was not unknown among sensitive dogs in the Territory.

Charles Pancoast, traveling through the desert with a group of forty-niners, remembered his companions suddenly shouting, "A river." The dogs had already spotted it and ran ahead. It turned out that all had been fooled by a mirage. The next day, when another similar mirage appeared, Pancoast said, "[O]ur poor dogs were again off in search of water."

When John Spring was still an Army sergeant during the 1850s, he and his unit left southern California on a 298-mile trek to the outpost in Yuma. On the twelfth night, Spring was kept awake by the dismal howling of coyotes, but he never expected one animal to dash into camp. The coyote pulled Spring's knapsack, with his canteen, out from under his head and dragged it away. Several others lost their canteens in the same way.

After recovering some of their belongings the next day, the men found themselves at the mercy of a sandstorm so blinding that they followed the wrong road for miles. By now, what water they had left had given out, and the water they found in holes was too alkaline to drink. A long detour around a steep ravine left them seriously dehydrated and exhausted, almost incapable of pushing through an a dense growth of prairie grass thickly layered with dust and sand.

VENISON STRIPS HUNG OUT TO DRY DURING A HUNTING TRIP IN THE CHIRICAHUA MOUNTAINS, ARIZONA TERRITORY.

One man, Cavanaugh, became deranged from heat and thirst, hallucinated, and finally fell dead. After burying him, the soldiers moved slowly on, knowing that the same was to happen to each of them if they didn't find water soon. When they at last reached the right road, they met another soldier who knew of a nearby river lagoon where they could drink the water.

Their good luck continued to hold when they met two Mexicans who carried five days' rations and cooked the unit a big meal. Once again, survival was through the kindness of strangers blessed with that "savage virtue."

CHAPTER THREE

Pulling Up Stakes

*As much a frontier icon as the log cabin, the tent
has been almost overlooked, yet settlers couldn't
have established Territorial towns without it.*

E XPLORING AND MAKING A LIVING IN THE SOUTHWEST DID
not mean, necessarily, that one was actually settling,
which individual shelters readily reflected. Even the
newcomer looking to put down roots in a particular locale often
lived a fairly nomadic life, especially if trying to dodge Apaches.
Nothing could be more suited to such frontier living than the
ever versatile tent. Whether the common A-frame type, the
wall tent, or the pyramidal, frontier tents served many purposes — a life-saving cover in severe storms, cheap outdoor
living for regaining one's health in a benign climate, a quickly
erected business when a mining camp boomed.

The soldier, the miner, the railroad builder, the itinerant
entrepreneur, and the footloose traveler all depended on tents
throughout Arizona's Territorial years. As late as the start of the
20th century, the construction camp for the future Roosevelt
Dam impressively displayed the useful diversity of such canvas shelters. Before buildings were erected there, tents housed
a field hospital, blacksmith and carpenter shops, main mess, and
sleeping quarters — a complete tent community.

Such diverse use guaranteed that tents varied from
lowlier styles to luxury class. In 1846, new bride Susan Shelby
Magoffin traveled the Santa Fe Trail with her husband from
Independence, Missouri, to what was then northern Mexico.

Samuel Magoffin was a successful merchant who cara-
vanned American goods to Santa Fe and other parts of Mexico.

Susan wrote in her journal that the couple slept each night in a "grand affair" of a tent:

> It is conical in shape, with an iron pole and wooden ball; we have a table in it that is fastened to the pole, and a little stand above it that serves for a dressing bureau — it holds our glass, combs, etc. Our bed is as good as many houses have . . . We have a carpet made of sail duck, have portable stools . . . This is certainly one of the "varieties of life" as well as of traveling. To be shut up in a carriage all day with a buffalo robe around you, and with the rain pouring down at 10 knots an hour. And at the close of this . . . I have books, writing implements, sewing, knit[t]ing, somebody to talk with, a house that does not leak, and I am satisfied . . .

At the other extreme were the simplest tents whose inhabitants suffered from the heat and cold. Even so, enterprising people learned how to lessen their discomfort. At Camp Lowell in Tucson, when summers heated a tent's interior unbearably, the soldiers copied local Indian peoples and built brush ramadas overhead as shade. During the winter, soldiers were known to dig trenches around their tents and bank the earth up around the sides as insulation.

Caught in a storm, an inventive group of miners improvised a stove by using a kerosene can and some old iron roofing fashioned into a stovepipe. "The storm lasted 36 hours, but owing to the natural genius of our crew, we had a really good time of it," one miner remembered.

When it came to keeping dry, a tent was as dependable as an adobe building, perhaps more so. The three-year-old adobe structures at Camp McDowell had, by 1869, become unsafe, largely from rain damage. The troops then lived in tents.

Baking sun, wintry cold, driving rain — and, of course, gusting winds. To break the force of the wind, one might wind a rope around the top of the tent and fasten it to a stake in the

**A NORTHERN ARIZONA INDIAN COUPLE
BY THEIR TENT, CIRCA 1906.**

ground, but a good enough blast could still topple a tent and force its residents into more drastic action.

One "bitterly cold" winter in the 1880s, a Mrs. Stillman had recently arrived in Bisbee, a copper-mining town set in a canyon of the Mule Mountains. "The wind never stopped blowing," she recalled, and if a miner's tent was blown down, he would quickly "wrap up in a blanket and crawl in with his neighbor."

Cowboy Earle Forrest remembered being tentless out on the range: "When we were out with the wagon, we had no tent or any place to keep dry when it rained or snowed. We just stood around the fire, which was pretty smoky with wet wood, and took it, or else went to bed and tried to imagine that we were dry."

Of course, even a good imagination can do only so much. Forrest would be just drifting off to sleep when the tarp and blanket beneath him would become soaked, and he would jerk awake with a start.

Tents naturally could be pitched almost anywhere, making them handy for many purposes. At the Columbia copper camp in the Helvetia District, a tent served as the official polling place in an 1882 election. Unfortunately, the election officers succumbed to temptation and left the tent to watch some nearby horse races. John Rockfellow had friends who were candidates, and when he saw that no one was overseeing the voting, he

**MAKESHIFT BUILDINGS COULD COMBINE BOARD
AND CANVAS, LIKE THIS TENT IN CROWN KING.**

was afraid that the precinct's votes might be disqualified. To protect against accusations of voter fraud, he organized a volunteer guard for the polling tent. The precinct's votes were indeed questioned, but because of the volunteers at the door, were finally accepted.

Like mushrooms, tent communities would sprout overnight — perhaps some prospector had suddenly struck it rich and everyone was rushing try his own luck, or perhaps a construction crew was laying track for the railroads. Inevitably, at least one tent would serve as a saloon, although drunken carousing could be much harder on a tent than on a wooden building. A saloon tent at the Silverbell mine was shot almost to tatters when a gunfight erupted between some Irishmen and some Mexicans, all thoroughly drunk.

As Arizona made a name for itself with its dry, healthful climate, tent camps became home for the rush of "health-seekers" who poured in from across the country. Rich and poor, they sought relief from tuberculosis and other often-fatal respiratory ailments and from painfully crippling afflictions like rheumatism and arthritis. These camps grew into sizable towns, one of the largest being "Bugville" near Tucson. People from all walks of life lived side by side — the poorer folks because tents provided affordable shelter, the well-to-do because doctors recommended tents as the ideal outdoor environment for recovery.

Established sanitoriums and boarding houses started putting up tents on their grounds. Tent housing became more and more sophisticated with the demand, offering advantages of indoor living as well outdoor living's promise of health. Specialized tents were designed, one of which allowed for air circulation in around the floor level and at at the top.

Gradually, the cost of medical help and conveniences that became the vogue at tent camps forced many of the more destitute to strike out on their own and keep moving around the empty desert stretches, either alone or with a few others. Beyond the bustle of the tent cities, the tents of these "desert rats" started dotting the landscape.

Books full of advice, like George Price's *Gaining Health in the West*, were written for the health-seeker. People were cautioned not to rely solely on tent living for their recovery — an adequate diet, exercise, and rest were essential, too. Still, when medical practices of the 1890s and early 1900s could offer little else for treating tuberculosis (the disease was not curable until after the 1944 discovery of the antibiotic streptomyocin), tent therapy caught and held the attention of the desperate.

When George Smalley, a young journalist living Arizona Territory, was reduced to skin and bones from overwork, but resisted taking any pills, his doctor advised him to live in a tent with a ramada attached and to adopt a new routine: "Each morning take a pail of water . . . pour it over your body, rubbing yourself vigorously for five to 10 minutes. Then exercise — run, grub, anything to keep in motion."

Smalley's doctor also told him to ride horseback, keep out of the sun, drink plenty of milk, and eat a pound of butter a day. On this regimen, the young man gained 40 pounds in four months and was healthy once more.

Of course, tents saw their share of human drama. Swiss-born John Spring was university educated and eventually taught school in Tucson, but before that he was a sergeant with the Arizona Regulars. In 1866, Spring was stationed at a new camp on the upper San Pedro River. Ordered to take a

**A TRAVELING PHOTOGRAPHER
BY HIS PLACE OF BUSINESS, CIRCA 1890.**

detail of 10 soldiers to scout for Apaches, he and his men were exploring a ravine near the camp's eastern edge.

Suddenly, Spring wrote later, "there rang out through the silence of the night, a fearful cry of 'Help,' emanating from a woman's throat."

The sergeant ran quickly up an incline to the Snarley family's tent and saw Mrs. Snarley — a hard-working woman with a worthless husband — "standing in partial undress in front of her bed, while her husband with fury in his eyes held his bayonet poised over her naked throat and bosom. . . . I struck the miscreant a violent blow upon the top of his head with the hilt of my sword; he fell like an ox struck by the butcher's pole-ax."

Spring carried the unconscious man to a bed and began to apply cold water to his wound, but the night's excitement was far from over. Mrs. Snarley, now seeing her husband "inert, bloody, and pale, . . . made a grab for the frying pan and howling at me, 'You have murdered my 'Arry,' struck me over the head with the red-hot cooking utensil. . . . The sizzling grease spread over my face," Spring recalled, "nearly blinding me. . . . [I]t was said afterward that I looked very 'comical.' I believe it, for I know I felt very 'comical.'"

'Twixt Barrel Cactus and Bear Jaws

*Worse than being caught between a rock
and a hard place, this spiky dilemma
hints at the following tales of dramatic escapes
and bare-knuckled endurance.*

———◆———

IN TERRITORIAL DAYS, WHEN CLOSE CALLS WERE COMMON-place, Gus Hickey's experience still made a good tale. He was just happy to be able to tell it. While camping in the Guadalupe Mountains in December 1890, Hickey and cowboys "Bunk" Robinson and Jack Bridges were attacked by Indians. After hours spent lurking behind rocks, Robinson moved and was shot dead in the head. Hickey jumped up and made a run for it. With bullets whizzing around him, he escaped, but not before, "one shot knocked off his hat and another cut off part of his hair."

Even luckier was the man in Show Low in the 1880s. A bullet pierced his scalp but lay against his skull without penetrating further. For an anesthetic, amateur surgeon C.E. Cooley administered doses of whiskey, then successfully removed the bullet.

If the stakes were high enough, a man might take a calculated risk with his life. Such a man was Fred Maish, owner of big ranches along the Santa Cruz. One time, when he had delivered a herd of cattle to Fort Grant, he was paid in gold pieces which he tied to himself. On the way home, he found the Gila River flooded. His horse went under, and he was weighted down by the gold and unable to swim. Unwilling to give up the gold, he survived by making his way out along the river bottom. Determination and luck had saved him.

Sometimes the odds were so overwhelming that there was no chance of saving both life and fortune. This was the situation when wagon-master Castenada, 14 men, nine wagons, and 80 mules, en route to Fort Grant, were attacked by about 200 Apaches in May 1869. Quickly pulling the wagons into a circle, Castenada and his men held out for 10 hours. With three men dead and his ammunition almost spent, he had still not surrendered when seven cavalry men suddenly came to his aid. But meanwhile the ranks of the Apache had swelled by another hundred. After a time, the ammunition again began to run out and, in order to save their lives, Castenada and the sergeant in command were forced to abandon the wagons and goods. The loss to merchants Tully and Ochoa was $12,000 and to the United States government too a sizeable sum.

Often, only fast thinking saved the day. In an effort to get his hands on $700 belonging to Ed Lumley and Tom Childs, the men's cook added strychnine to their food. As their stomachs began to spasm, Childs realized what had happened. He and Lumley drained the oil from the sardine cans, swallowed it, threw up the poison, and averted certain death.

Quick-witted thinking also saved Dr. John Lacy, physician in charge of the Arizona Copper Company Hospital in the 1880s. The doctor was accustomed to traveling between the neighboring mining towns of Clifton and Morenci by using a velocipede on the narrow-gauge railroad track. One day Lacy came face to face with a train engine. Sizing up his predicament, he leapt from his vehicle and landed in the river, his velocipede following shortly. Neither man nor conveyance was injured, only bruised, according to the newspaper account.

Savvy old rancher and Indian fighter Pete Kitchen had to call on his long experience while he was out hunting Apaches with some Army officers. When he became separated from the other men, a number of Indians set out after him. Outnumbered and outpaced, Kitchen swiftly assessed his plight. Reaching into his pocket, he removed some blocks of "California matches"and tore off one at a time. Scratching them on the bottom of his stirrup, he lit one after another. As they hit the grass, a fire flared up. The Indians wisely gave up the chase.

Many a time a man owed his life not to luck or his own quick wits but to the timely intervention of an animal. Once rancher John Rockfellow was trudging up a steep slope on his return from Portrero with his burros loaded with mail and supplies. At the same moment that his burros strayed off the trail, a huge brown bear suddenly came lumbering down the path toward him. Man and bear stopped in their tracks and regarded each other. Rockfellow reached for his revolver, although he knew it was inadequate against the enormous animal. At that moment his burro, Balaam, curious but unafraid, let out a "friendly bray" from behind. Terrified, the bear raced toward Rockfellow and, crowding him aside, disappeared down the trail. Rockfellow rushed after him and was in time to see the big creature lose control and roll hundreds of feet into a gulch. With only his dignity injured, the bear picked himself up and sped off.

When a crowd was bent on lynching, the alleged offender was usually destined to die within hours if not minutes. In 1880s Flagstaff a young railroad worker thought it was fun to see how close he could shoot at an 80-man construction crew without actually hitting anyone. Tiring of this "game," the crew locked the fellow into a boxcar with the intention of hanging him after supper. As they were about to string him up, one man among them drew his guns and threatened to kill as many as he could if they insisted on the hanging. At last, 14 others joined in and persuaded the crowd to release the young man if he would go East the next morning. Needing no urging, the rash young man left in haste, having experienced the dubious pleasures of a close call.

Many a close call meant not simply a slight brush with danger but a face-to-face collision with death. Sergeant Anson, stationed at Fort Huachuca in 1890, went deer hunting, but became separated from his companions.

**FOOTING COULD BE TRICKY ON STEEP, ROCKY TRAILS —
A PACK TRAIN THREADS CANYON DIABLO.**

He made his way alone to a spring that he knew that deer came to. After a bit, a deer did step up to the spring, and Anson knelt down to watch it, completely unaware of the bear quietly approaching from him behind.

Apparently protecting her nearby cubs, the bear leaped on Anson's right leg, mutilating it. Then, rising up, with one claw she swept away his gun and planted the claws of her other foot squarely in his face.

For just an instant the bear pulled back, but then came on again, jaws open. Unable to reach his knife, Anson forced his right arm into the bear's throat. Its teeth closed tightly around his arm, but, using great strength, Anson held her paws away from him. Man and bear hit the ground and rolled together to the bottom of the hill.

All this time Anson had been shouting for desperately for help. When his alarmed companions finally appeared on the run, the bear let go of Anson, lumbered up the hill, grabbed his gun in her teeth, and disappeared into the bush. Anson survived with a badly scarred face and mutilated arm and leg.

The Penningtons are honored for being the first family of United States citizenship to settle in Arizona, as well as for their courage in the face of repeated Apache attacks. But in a family history long on close calls, most notable is Larcena's story.

Elias and Julia Pennington, originally of the Carolinas, first moved to Tennessee, where Larcena was born in 1837, followed by a brother and sister. After five years in Tennessee, the family moved on to Texas for 15 years. There the rest of the 12 children were born — three more boys and six more girls — before Julia Pennington died in 1857. The restless Elias and his 12 children joined a wagon train for California.

Their exhausted cattle and Larcena's "mountain fever" forced the family to stop at Fort Buchanan. From then on, the Pennington destinies were to be linked with Arizona. During their two years at the fort, Elias and his sons supported the family by whipsawing logs, while the daughters sewed for Army wives. In December 1859, Larcena married lumberman John Hempstead Page. Larcena and John became the first American couple to be married in Tucson, a town that had belonged first to Spain and then Mexico.

Three months later, Page was employed by William Kirkland as a lumberman working in the Santa Rita Mountains. Larcena joined him and frontiersman William Randall at their camp, along with Mercedes Dias, Kirkland's 11-year-old Mexican ward. It seemed an ideal arrangement, since Kirkland was anxious for Larcena to tutor Mercedes.

One morning both Page and Randall set out from the camp, leaving Larcena and Mercedes alone — despite Kirkland's stated uneasiness about the Apache situation. Page went to secure some tools, Randall to track down a deer.

As Larcena was about to fetch water to do a wash, she heard Mercedes scream that Apaches were coming. Retrieving a six-shooter from under the bedcovers, Larcena recalled, "I turned to fire at them – but before I could pull the trigger, they had rushed upon me."

She screamed, but was quickly silenced when the Indians "struck me with their lances, and told us to keep quiet or they would kill us." Adding to her horror, one Apache, who spoke a

LARCENA PENNINGTON PAGE SCOTT,
FIRST FROM TENNESSEE AND THEN
FROM TEXAS, TENACIOUSLY MADE HER
OWN PLACE IN ARIZONA HISTORY.

little Spanish, told her that they had just killed her husband. Next, the Indians looted the camp.

Despite Larcena's weakened condition — she wasn't fully recovered from a bout of "fever and ague" — the Indians tried to forced her and Mercedes to walk fast. They covered about 16 miles by Larcena's estimate. But when her strength failed her, the Indians took her shoes and all her clothes except for a single garment, stabbed her with their lances — she told of receiving 11 wounds to her back, arms, and head — threw her over a cliff about 16 feet high, and hurled huge stones at her.

By her own reckoning, Larcena lay unconscious in a snowbank for about three days. At last, so weak from loss of blood that she could scarcely stand, she began her long trek back to the little cabin. Eating only wild onions and seeds and drinking snow water, she struggled along for the next 10 days, not daring to follow a trail for fear of the Indians finding her.

Her sufferings can scarcely be grasped from her brief description: "My feet gave out the first day and I was compelled to crawl the most of the distance. . . . Sometimes after crawling up a steep ledge, laboring hard for half a day, I would lose my footing and slide down lower than the place from which I started — I was at a point said to be 6,000 feet above the sea and only wonder that I did not freeze."

Years later, she told her son-in-law that "her feet became filled with small stones; her bare shoulders were blistered with the hot sun; her head was a mass of clotted blood." At night, unable to rest on her wounded back, she would crouch on all fours and dream of food. Then, taking her direction from the sun each day, she would move south until she came at last to a ridge overlooking Madera Canyon.

Two days later, she reached the vacant teamster camp and, finding a campfire still burning low, retrieved a stick burning at one end and carried it to her husband's old camp close by. She ate and drank a little, bathed her wounds, and slept there that night. The next morning on the road to a nearby camp, she was seen at last. An Englishman, who saw her later in Tucson, spoke of her "sunken temples, the lips drawn so tightly over the jaw that each tooth could be easily counted through them, the arms scarcely larger than a man's thumb, and the continuous cry for food."

John Page heard of his wife's return just as he was about to set out on his third rescue effort. Young Mercedes was eventually returned in exchange for some Apache prisoners.

The drama of Larcena's life was far from over. A year later, when Larcena was three months pregnant, Apaches did kill her husband as he was traveling to Camp Grant. After their daughter, Mary, was born, Larcena went to live with her family in the stone house on the Santa Cruz.

Before long, she again was forced to flee from the Apaches with her baby, taking refuge in the fortified Mowry Mine. When a smallpox epidemic broke out there, both she and Mary were stricken.

Miraculously surviving mine owner Sylvester Mowry's bread-and-water "cure," Larcena and baby Mary returned to share the family's fortunes on its frequent moves over the next years,

**U.S. ARMY AMBULANCE AND DRIVER
AT FORT APACHE, ARIZONA TERRITORY.**

1862 to 1869. Like other families, the Penningtons went wherever they could earn a living while trying to avoid Apache attack.

As freighters, the Pennington men spent long periods on the road with their great wagons and teams of 12 to 14 oxen, leaving the women to cope alone with the ever-present Apache threat. In 1864, a visitor to Tubac reported the village abandoned except for the Pennington women, their two young brothers, and Larcena's daughter, Mary. Every morning the two little boys "with guns as long as themselves, carefully reconnoitered each side of the path to the spring from which the women then carried the water supply for the day."

Ann Pennington died in 1867 of malaria. The next year brother Jim was killed by Apaches while he was pursuing them to recover oxen stolen from his camp near Tucson. Only a year later, in 1869, Apaches killed Elias and Larcena's favorite brother, Green — Elias while plowing a field and Green while trying to save his father, not knowing he was already dead. That same year, Ellen died of pneumonia as the family was about to leave for California.

Five dead in three years. Brother Jack came to take the remaining Penningtons back to Texas. All except Larcena. She chose to stay in Arizona and married Judge William F. Scott in

1870. She lived the rest of her life quietly in Tucson, dying there in 1913 at the age of 76.

This apparently frail young woman with her recurrent fevers survived a brutal attack and near starvation to overcome grief, bear a child, battle smallpox, remarry, and enjoy a serene old age, outliving many in her large family and seeing Arizona Territory achieve statehood.

Raphael Pumpelly provided a final surprising glimpse of her. Stopping at the Pennington home on the Santa Cruz a few months after Larcena's ordeal with the Apaches, he recorded her story, adding: "I was told that the first thing she asked for [on her return to civilization] was tobacco, which she was in the habit of chewing."

Hospitals did exist in Territorial Arizona, but often treatment might have to be improvised on the spot, whether the emergency involved childbirth, gunshot, or disease. Where someone with formal medical training was usually hard — even impossible — to find, a patient might have to rely on a willing bystander with guts, ingenuity, and wit. Dr. Joseph H. Bill, for instance, once had to use "both knees as a counter-force against an arrowhead embedded in the humurus." Another surgeon conducted an operation while sitting on a tree stump with his patient across a whisky barrel. The heat, dust, and flies were intolerable, he later recalled.

When it came to ingenuity, it was hard to beat some of the contract surgeons the Army hired for $125 a month. Dr. Corbusier was sent to the Verde River Indian Agency in 1872 to treat malaria. He faced the problem of efficiently dispensing limited quantities of quinine and bismoth subnitrites, so Corbusier asked the medicine men to administer the medicine as they performed their rituals and incantations.

At Fort McDowell where soldiers were subsisting on nothing but beans and coffee, another Army physician made up for the men's dietary deficiency by collecting watercress along the riverbank.

**DR. C.E. YOUNT PUT
HIS MICROSCOPE —
AND HIS WITS —
TO GOOD USE.**

Just fulfilling the routine jobs required at each Army post
was difficult enough to keep the medical officer busy. Among
other chores, he had to keep a daily log of the weather, sickness,
births, deaths, and sanitary conditions, in addition to inspect-
ing the solders' quarters and the food.

Doctors might even need to be astute enough to detect
fraud. At Fort Lowell in 1876, when Private Kelly's diarrhea
persisted despite the best efforts of Dr. Walter Reed — later famous for his research with yellow fever — Reed finally discovered that Kelly was eating soap every day to stay ill and
avoid being sent back to duty.

Another fraud involved a prostitute in 1903 Prescott.
Afraid that the two men who had brought her there were losing
interest, she faked a hemorrhage and called on Dr. C. E. Yount
for help. He arrived to find both the patient and her bed covered
with blood, but no other signs of illness. Suspicious, Young put
a sample of the blood under his microscope. The shape of the
blood cells confirmed that the blood was that of a freshly slaugh-
tered sheep. Far from emerging with a reputation for astute

detective work, poor Yount was threatened by the prostitute's two companions and laughed up and down Whisky Row.

Physicians had to depend on bystanders for help. Ralph Palmer was chief surgeon when the Roosevelt Dam was under construction about 1900. After a spinal needle broke off in a patient who moved unexpectedly, Dr. Palmer used Tommy, "a mess hall flunky," to administer chloroform while he removed the needle fragment. Eventually, because of heavy demands made on him, Palmer hired a man named Bush who claimed he had been a hospital steward although he had "all the appearance of a genuine tramp."

Martha Summerhayes wrote that when they were living at the desolate post of Ehrenberg, her husband encouraged a steamboat agent with slight medical experience to extract a tooth for a suffering young woman. "Fisher took up the forceps and clattered around amongst Ellen's sound white teeth. His hand shook, great beads of perspiration gathered on his face, and I perceived a very strong odor of Cocomonga wine. It was, however, too late to protest. He fastened on a molar, and with the lion's strength which lay in his gigantic frame, he wrenched it out. Ellen put up her hand and felt the place. 'My God, You've pulled the wrong tooth!' cried she, and so he had."

Despite occasional examples of gross ineptitude, self-trained healers gave invaluable help at a time when there were few others at hand. Engineer Raphael Pumpelly and Hiram Washburn were traveling in Apacheland when Washburn accidentally shot himself in the thigh. A knowledgeable old Spaniard, who happened to be in the vicinity, cut out the ball, and some kind Mexican women nursed Washburn until he was healed.

Joe Burgano owed his life to the remarkable Joe Axford, steward at the Tombstone Hospital. Hit on the head by a rock while working in the Black Diamond Mine in the Dragoon Mountains, Burgano was rushed to the Tombstone Hospital with a severely fractured skull. Shattered bone fragments were actually "showing in the brain material which was already oozing out of the wound." Both the regular surgeon and his substitute were away at the time. Another doctor, although not a surgeon, said he would step in, but when it quickly became clear that he was not equal to the job, Axford took over. Up to this point, Axford's sole training had consisted of watching the regular surgeon, Dr. Bacon, perform a similar operation, explaining as he worked how much pressure to exert with the saw and how to avoid hitting the large artery. Axford must have been an apt pupil because Burgano recovered, except that his pulse was always visible in his right temple where the opening had been made.

In the Territory, 21 women were registered as physicians, although few lived there long. But hundreds more acted as midwives, and some women without formal training were referred to as doctors. Before the community of Mayer had a physician, Joe Mayer said of petite, red-haired Sadie, "my wife is as good as a doctor . . . she has the gift." She set bones, removed steel splinters from the eyes of miners, and once nursed a hotel full of smallpox patients with the help of only three assistants.

The lasting gratitude of Sadie Mayer's patients was matched by what some Apaches felt toward Cordelia Crawford. While waging a war of extermination against other settlers around the Crawford ranch, the Apaches left the Crawfords untouched because of how Cordelia doctored the Apache women and their children.

Short, squarely-built Hester Skaggs Rudy, of Yavapai County, bore children, planted crops, held off hostile Indians with a rifle, and acted as doctor and midwife for many in the community. In that same area, Josephine Shupp helped the sick, too, often traveling at night to reach a patient and always taking along "a jar of jelly or a pail of broth."

Most babies in the Territory were born at home, and many were delivered by midwives. During Prescott's first 50 years, the town leaned heavily on her grandmother, Dora Lee Sessions remembered. A midwife for virtually all the births in town, Dora Lee's grandmother was a no-nonsense realist whose advice when her small granddaughter hurt herself one day was, "It will be all

**NURSE GWENDOLYN WRENALL ROCKS
INFANT JOHN THOMAS RIGDEN IN
KIRKLAND, ARIZONA TERRITORY, 1911.**

right by the time you get married." Oddly enough, despite the
midwives' "timid" use of water and lack of antiseptics or even
"reasonable cleanliness, there were few ill aftereffects."

Physicians often exhibited quirky behavior suited to the
rough and ready environment. Known in Prescott for his battle-
scarred face, full beard, and constant swearing, Dr. Warren
Day was one such character. Once, when he was riding in his
buggy, it somehow came apart in the middle. Rather than drop
the reins, the redoubtable doctor jumped forward onto the axle
of the front wheels and rode them down the hill, swearing at top
volume all the way.

Dr. John Flinn, thin and frail, had journeyed to the
Southwest for his health. While in Kingman one night, he was
prevailed upon by mining engineer Otto Kuencer to aid Mrs.
Kuencer, who was in labor. Dr. Flinn jumped out of bed and

DOCTORS REACHED THEIR PATIENTS BY ANY MEANS THEY COULD — DR. CONRAD IN HIS BUGGY, 1876.

tried to keep up with the speeding Kuencer as he ran across town lots. When Flinn's strength gave out, he let Kuencer carry him the rest of the way to his home. World reknowned by this time for his tuberculosis sanitorium, Dr. Flinn obviously did not suffer from an exaggerated sense of dignity.

Nor did Dr. Benjamin Moeur, who, in order to reach a patient on the other side of the Roosevelt Dam, rode across in a cement bucket.

Something of both the hilarious aspect of that era in Arizona history and of the memorable qualities of men and women who practiced medicine is captured in an anecdote Dr. Jack McDonnell told about himself. One time, he recalled, he operated on the nearly severed toe of a miner: "I sewed it back on, and it grew just fine. The only thing was, I sewed it on upside down."

In a land rife with quirky characters, Burro Frenchy was in a class by himself. But if people thought him odd, they gave him even a little more license than most, because Frenchy's close calls would make anyone a little touched. And no one could question his guts.

Born Claude Batailleur, Frenchy had served as a corporal in Louis Napolean's army and been decorated for bravery. Before leaving Paris for the United States, he'd established a laundry company and had even gotten elected king of the annual laundry festival.

Frenchy brought his keen business sense to Arizona Territory in 1876, where he developed and traded mining claims. But his conversational mixture of "profanity, French, bad Spanish, and worse English, with a few words of Apache thrown in," earned him a reputation as an eccentric. Not to say that his fiery temperament and an affinity for burros and mules didn't help, too. Burro Frenchy anecdotes abounded and were recorded by writer and artist Ross Santee, who even interviewed Frenchy in later life.

There was the time he shot a dog that attacked the burro he was riding. When the dog's owner sued, Frenchy hired a lawyer, but then did all the talking himself in his weird mix of languages. At last he stopped ranting, and his lawyer said, "After all, Mr. Batailleur, you shot in self-defense."

"No fence," responded Frenchy. "Open country everywhere. No shoot him in ze fence . . . !," and before his lawyer could intervene, Frenchy had announced that he shot the dog as it was running away. The court fined both Frenchy and his lawyer.

His set-to with the bear added to the legend. He was on his way back to his cabin after a night of drinking. Suddenly, a bear loomed before him. Thinking it was a man blocking his path, he yelled, "Out of my way," and let loose with a punch. The bear responded by knocking Frenchy cold. Some miners found him lying in the path the next morning. He was hurt, but very much alive.

The Apaches spared people they considered crazy, and since Frenchy had them and everyone else convinced that he was, they let him be . . . until Frenchy went into partnership with a Mexican on a ranch stocked with hogs near present-day

**A SOLITARY, RAGTAG PROSPECTOR
HAD TO RELY ON HIMSELF AND HIS BURROS.**

Solomon, New Mexico. The Apache hatred for hogs was well known, and they promptly attacked the ranch.

Frenchy escaped, but they caught him and gave him a 24-hour chance to get away. After a desperate all-night run, he was caught again. The Apaches stripped him, lashed him with cactus stalks and whips, beat him with clubs, and even chopped pieces from his back, before finally hanging him head down over a slow fire. Then the women started skinning him.

Somehow still alive and conscious, Frenchy calculated that his only chance lay in persuading the Apaches that he was totally mad. Tossing back his head, he barked like a coyote, then crawled like a snake, and finished the show by roaring and charging at them like a grizzly. Convinced beyond doubt "that they had harmed a blighted one, the Apaches fled in terror."

Frenchy survived the torture, but with a battered body that he had to drag along and a voice so out of control that he terrified everyone within hearing as he bellowed to his mules.

Eccentric and disfigured he might be, but Burro Frenchy had proved that he was far from crazy. An old Globe prospector, watching Frenchy slowly inch his way up the street, gave the fairest assessment of him: "Take a long look, cowdogs. That hombre is all man."

CHAPTER FIVE

Strange Friends
in Lonely Places

*Even when an individualist needed to roam a land
with no fences, no mortgages, and no taxes,
he still wanted someone to come home to.*

———◆———

W ITH THE NEAREST NEIGHBOR AT LEAST A DAY'S TRAVEL
away and the nearest saloon even farther, a lonely
prospector or homesteader had few options for company. Utter loneliness drove some men crazy. They might not see
another human being for weeks, maybe months, and even attack-
ing Apaches tended to bombard their targets from out of sight.

Carl Ryan, a sociable Irishman ranching in the Patagonia
Mountains during the 1880s, welcomed whatever occasional
company dropped by his place. For his day-to-day solace, however, Ryan depended on Dick, the friendly pig who followed at
his heels, every now and then giving an amiable grunt.

One Army officer took comfort in the gift of a number of
quail — not in eating them, but by keeping them as pets. He
reared them to eat from his hand and wrote that he loved their
"pranks and quarrels . . . [they're] so tame and confiding, even rec-
ognizing my voice and responding to my call when I am out of
sight." As an experiment, he let two birds go. They returned,
but not alone, bringing numerous "friends" from the wild, until the
lieutenant found that it took an entire biscuit for their daily rations.

Pioneer Horatio Farrar also found companionship in an
unlikely source. On a hunting expedition with a friend in New
Mexico Territory in the early 1870s, Farrar returned to camp
to hear mysterious scratchings coming from his food bin. He

61

**IN DESERT EXTREMES, EVEN DOGS
GOT TO RIDE RATHER THAN WALK.**

discovered a hungry black bear cub, which he tooke home and raised to be a cherished pet, always ready to tumble and frolic. Farrar's bear was, in his owner's estimation, at least as intelligent as the average dog.

Cats, too, help fill the lonely void. Alone for a time in Pinal in the early 1900s, Dane Coolidge welcomed the company of a little yellow cat. After he killed a coyote that was harassing the cat, the feline became his close companion. It followed him everywhere and slept on his bed at night.

Dogs were not only amusingly eccentric company in their own doggy way, but could prove quite helpful. John Rockfellow's bull terrier Patches specialized in snakes. The dog could tell if a snake was poisonous or not and then treated it accordingly. A harmless snake he would grab in the middle and shake until he bit the reptile in two. With rattlesnakes, Patches would bark and charge from a distance until at last the snake turned tail to flee. Only then would the dog pounce, snapping the snake's head off.

Diverting but decidely less useful was John Rockfellow's burro. To make ready for a 400-mile trip, he and his group spent one day preparing beef jerky and haging it out on lines to dry. With a shotgun at the ready in case of night intruders, Rockfellow was asleep when a commotion began. After hurriedly making sure that the noise wasn't from one of his traveling companions, Rockfellow shot in the general direction of the disturbance.

A terrible braying filled the night. Rockfellow had pumped quail-shot into the side of the thief — his own pack burro, John Daisy. The opportunistic burro already had a reputation for stealing anything from tin cans to soup and that night had found it couldn't resist the allure of fresh beef jerky. The burro still made the trip, but with its wounds carefully bandaged and its pack considerably lightened.

F rontier animal companions often displayed a loyalty to their humans that went much deeper than just waiting for the next meal. A detail from Fort Apache in September 1881, after an Indian attack on the post, came upon the bodies of four men and six horses. Standing guard over his dead master was a great mastiff, half-crazed from over a week without water. Once given a drink, he became fairly friendly. Even so, he had to be taken away, howling mournfully, from the spot where his master had lain.

A comparable incident occurred many years before at the junction of the Gila and Colorado Rivers in November 1849. There, Lieutenant Whipple wrote of "a poor dog that nightly howls the requiem of his drowned master," — a Mexican boy — weeks after the event.

John Spring, soldier and later Tucson schoolmaster, owed his life to a dog that had just befriended him. On their way to Tubac in November of 1868, Spring and two companions, Hamlin and Ramon, were camping near the Santa Rita Mountains when a very lean hunting dog appeared and looked hungrily at their frying bacon. After a good supper, the dog settled himself close to Spring. Up at 10 P.M., Spring took his turn keeping watch, for Indian danger was high at that time. When it was the hour for Hamlin to take the next watch, Spring had trouble rousing him because he had been drinking, but Spring finally got him up and warned him that the dog was acting uneasy.

About an hour and a half later, Spring was wakened by the dog jerking frantically at his overcoat and barking. He jumped up, gun in hand, as did Ramon. Hamlin, their watch, slept on in a drunken stupor. When daylight came, the men discovered Indian tracks within 40 feet of their camp. The hunting dog had befriended them just in time to save their lives.

Spring rewarded the dog with a sumptuous breakfast and a hug. Later that day, Spring went bird-hunting and the stray followed. Perhaps he was a little too eager for the hunt, but the dog ran between Spring's legs, tripping him and causing the gun to fire accidentally. Violently annoyed, Spring lashed out and kicked the dog. The dog ran off, never to return, and Spring sorely regretted his angry impulse.

When Harry Lee was living alone at an isolated ranch about 10 miles from Prescott in the 1860s, a stranger left a pregnant old yellow hound with him, swearing she was trained to always growl, not bark, "if redskins is anywhere about." A few days later Old Fan presented Lee with a litter of two puppies. Not long after she woke him one night by "pushing her nose into his face . . . growling low in her throat" and then running out toward the potato patch and back. Grabbing his shotgun and revolver, Lee ran for the tunnel he'd dug for just an emergency. When the moon rose, he peered out the peephole and shot at several dark moving shapes. "Several of the raiders burst out of the potato patch like a covey of startled quail, with Old Fan and her pups right at their heels."

In 1870s Tombstone, dogs were scarce, highly valued, and often stolen. Miners living on the outskirts of town depended on their barking to warn of approaching Apaches. But just a few years later, Tombstone's dogs had so multiplied that a license tax was levied on all dogs, and unlicensed ones were to be impounded and killed.

Acquiring a stray dog became popular among lonely soldiers posted far from home. At Fort Bowie, near the Chiricahua

FEEDING THE HOGS BY THE TEWKSBURY CABIN. (THIS PHOTOGRAPH WAS SHOT NOT LONG AFTER THE CLOSE OF THE PLEASANT VALLEY WAR.)

Mountains, many men of the 6th Cavalry kept dogs as pets, in addition to the ones owned by the New Mexican Volunteers.

All might have gone well with this mix of men and dogs had not a drum major decided to teach bugle calls to two New Mexican Volunteer buglers. After days of practice away from camp, the drum major announced that he was ready "to perform a retreat at the close of the usual sunset parade. But . . . as soon as the bugles started to give forth sounds that seemed to come forth from the subterranean caverns of the damned, all the dogs in the immediate vicinity, about 30, squatted on their haunches and broke forth in the most heartrending howls . . . the commanding officer turned purple with fury."

With the Army's dignity at stake, the drum major was demoted and the dogs were shot, except for a mastiff and two hunting dogs.

"Canning" dogs enjoyed a vogue, as reported in a Phoenix paper: "A tin can with a dog fastened to it rushed down Monroe Street this morning. This is a very dangerous sport and should not be allowed, as a runaway of teams is generally the result."

In 1883, the 6th Cavalry moved to Fort Apache, together with the entire 6th Cavalry band. Their imposing dress parades were watched with great interest by the entire community, including wives, young lady visitors, and many Apaches. One summer evening, the band, led by the drum major, was passing in full glory when the telegraph office door flew open:

> [F]rom it burst a large, active Apache dog . . . leading a good-sized tin can which someone had fastened to his rather busy tail . . . The dog flew down that line of soldiers like a canine thunderbolt. . . . The animal dashed straight at the band, passing between the legs of the drum major, upsetting him in all his official and musical dignity, and plowing a groove through the massed musicians that completely broke up the formation and stopped all further musical efforts. The shrieks of laughter that rose from the onlookers woke the very echoes. A good time was had by all.

CHAPTER SIX

Small Fry

*Meals might run long on beans,
chores always had to be done, and the Apaches
never seemed to let up, but a frontier childhood
gave plenty of scope for mischief.*

———◆———

I T WAS CHRISTMAS EVE IN TOMBSTONE, ARIZONA TERRITORY, in the early 1880s when a group of boys, self-styled the "Dirty Dozen," discovered a stray steer wandering around on West Freemont Street. Chasing him uptown, they eventually roped and tied him in front of the Can Can Café, to the entertainment of assorted drunk miners and cowboys.

"Tie a can to his tail," one of the drunks shouted, but Kats Woods, son of a local banker, went him one better and tied on some firecrackers instead. When they exploded between the steer's legs, it jumped about 10 feet and plunged through the plate glass window of the Can Can. Inside the café, the convivial Christmas atmosphere was shattered and a female dishwasher rushed outside, yelling, "It's the Devil, it's the Devil."

Life could be on the wild side for youngsters growing up in Territorial days, especially in the Territory's earlier years. Scarcely surprising, considering the primitive state of the schools, the rudimentary justice system, and the hit-or-miss law enforcement in some communities.

"Many times," Jennie Parks Ringgold remembered, her "father and mother were complimented in later years on their extraordinary family of [five] sons, extraordinary because they were raised in the early days when the West was Wild . . . and life was in the rough. . . . [Yet] all came through with clean records." Through the 1880s, the Parks family lived in Duncan.

**CHARLES STRAUSS JR. AND HIS
FATHER IN A DASHING FRONTIER POSE.**

During Tombstone's heyday, the Dirty Dozen lived up to their name with many escapades. One was their effort to rid the town of Chinese laundry men. Seeing themselves as champions of a poor laundress, Ma Holland, whose business had slacked off, they decided to wage a rotten-egg-and-tomato campaign against the Chinese competition. This war ended after they threw rocks through the windows of a Chinese laundry.

The next day in school it appeared that their teacher, Professor Metcalf, had heard about the incident. After a verbal whiplashing, he let loose with a willow switch on the Dirty Dozen's president, whereupon he was attacked by the entire group. One boy threw an ink bottle, cutting Metcalf on the head, while another took a baseball bat and knocked him out. This was a punishable offense, even in Tombstone, and Harry Hughes, the only "gang" member not rounded up by the police, wisely fled town until the furor had died down.

Many boys in Tombstone at the time thought of themselves as men before they had reached their teens, according to historian John Myers. Especially those living on ranches, "did a man's work and went around armed like men; and they were outraged when teachers objected to this practice in class rooms."

The use of firearms by youngsters was one ingredient that made life wilder for those growing up in the early days. Youthful cowboys and delinquent types weren't the only ones to tote them. They were part of life for ordinary kids, girls as well as boys. When Edith Stratton Kitt was a 10-year-old, her grandfather gave her a 10-gauge single-barrel shotgun. At that moment, hunting was added to horseback riding as a major interest for Edith. Her active frontier background comes through in her account of the time she shot at three teal ducks swimming in a row:

> I wounded them all, and after thinking that I had successfully wrung their necks, I packed them home behind me. When Mother asked me what I was holding behind me, I proudly threw them down in front. One lay still, one ran under the house, and the third started to flutter off but the dog caught it. Mother stuffed all three with onions and we had roast duck for supper.

Despite the relatively free life that Edith Stratton Kitt — like other girls of the time — led on the Southwest frontier, she realized later how much she had missed "by not being a cowboy among cowboys." Girls might be allowed to ride and hunt, but it was usually the boys who found "adventure everywhere," as one of them later remembered.

Nor did children who grew up in towns miss out on guns and hunting. Gail Gardner, raised in Prescott, wrote of killing quail on Washington Street and "plenty of doves on the thistle covered flats" now the city ball park and playground. When he and his friends lacked ammunition, they resorted to slingshots for hunting rabbits. "A sturdy fork, very strong rubber

**MISS LOUISE GIBBS DISPLAYS
HER DOVE-HUNTING PROWESS.**

bands, a leather pocket and you were in business." Sometimes
they shot "iron slugs out from the ends of horse shoes . . . a
more lethal weapon could hardly be imagined."

As the century wore on, guns were less in evidence and
much "delinquent" behavior became more like hi-jinks. When cir-
cuses and fairs became yearly events, for instance, getting in il-
legally just added to the fun. Boys would "hide outside the
main tent until the guard had passed and then slip under the
canvas. We would find ourselves in a dark cavern-like place
under the bleachers, with hundreds of legs dangling down."
The rest was easy. They would start "tapping men's legs and
soon a hand would reach down to pull one of us up to a seat
alongside our benefactor."

To get into the annual fair, boys took to standing on each
others' backs to get over the fence. If caught, "a boy would be
marched into the county court house, lectured and finally re-
leased," — only to try again, since no one regarded these youthful pranks very seriously.

Some escapades seemed harmless but generated acute anxiety for the parents. One incident that took place along the Salt River involved several of the 10 sons of Daniel and Mary Ellen Jones. On a day when the river was tumultuous from a heavy rain, the Joneses discovered that their boys were missing.

The worried father first found their "barefooted tracks" and then their clothes hidden in a clump of bushes. At last, hearing their voices, he "found a lot of naked little boys just getting out of the water. Each was dragging a two-inch plank." The boys had walked several miles up to the head of the canal and, then, getting hold of planks, had ridden them over the waves all the way downstream. "It was a trip many men in their right senses would hesitate to do," a newspaper account said.

Holidays like the Fourth of July provided more opportunities for dangerous antics. Kids could buy all kinds of fireworks including the awesome foot-long giant cannon cracker. Once, a small boy, having lit one of the giants, "accidentally" sent it through the door of a crowded saloon, where it exploded. Seconds later, the patrons came "boiling out [like a] swarm of yellow jackets."

For scamps like Jack O'Connor and his best friend, Gordon Goodwin, of Tempe, Halloween offered irresistible temptations. "We considered it a poor Hallow'en indeed if between us we didn't turn over 10 privies," Jack recalled. This once the two friends realized they had gone too far when they upset the privy belonging to the local Catholic church.

"The edifice had passed the point of no return when we heard a startled cry from within," the voice of the "ancient, scholarly and absent-minded" Spanish priest. "It was too late. All we could do was to run," Jack recalled.

But their Halloween prank was nothing compared to the skunk escapade. Jack and Gordon used to earn money by trapping skunks and selling their pelts. On one occasion, they decided to save the contents of a full scent bag by pouring it into a bottle. "Then one of us got a brilliant idea. Here was the skunk scent. There was the school. The prank seemed ordained

**YOUNG HENRY LEVIN STANDS BY HIS
FATHER, ALEXANDER LEVIN.**

by a higher being. We opened a window, sneaked in and put a drop or two of essence on every eraser in the building."

Soon identified as the culprits, Jack and Gordon were ordered to perform a massive scrubbing effort. The smell remained. The school was ventilated and finally fumigated, but the smell persisted — for years. Heroes to the younger children, who enjoyed a week's vacation at the outset, the boys were the enemy of the principal and school board. "I never told the harried principal that he could solve his problems by getting rid of the erasers," the unregenerate Jack remembered.

Turn-of-the-century larks weren't known for subtle wit or tender care of animals. In 1898 Mesa, after the street lamps were first electrified, the bulbs drew thousands of June bugs. The bugs attracted a throng of large green frogs. Getting a package of cigarettes, the local boys "would light one and put it into a frog's mouth. . . . The frog would sit there and puff out the smoke until it got short and would burn his mouth."

By the end of the 19th century, activities that scarcely
would have been noticed 20 years earlier began to constitute
criminal behavior. "Any minor," read one 1893 ordinance, ". . .
who shall visit, hang around, or loiter in or about any . . . billiard
or drinking saloon, bar or other place where intoxicating liquors
are kept or sold or who shall loiter about any street corner or
private building without permission of the owners thereof . . .
shall be guilty of a misdemeanor."

Civilization had arrived in a hurry. Serious crimes like
murder had usually been dealt with summarily, but in the "good
old days," there had been a certain tolerance toward youthful
waywardness. Now, delinquent youngsters could no longer hope
for the charitable attitude shown one young offender in
Tombstone in 1887. The landlady of a "beardless youth," who
had stolen money from her, made the following statement to
the grand jury: "Gentlemen, don't be hard on the poor little fellow. He robbed me, but I forgive him. He is young and inexpe-
rienced, and besides that, Gentlemen, he could not help it,
Gentlemen, for he comes from Texas."

The early Southwest, especially through the eyes of a mother
ushering her children to a new, yet-unseen home, could
seem less than promising. Estella Kentfield Colton and her two
small children left California in 1887 to join her husband in
Florence, Arizona Territory, a train trip she remembered in her
1935 memoirs: "On our way between Los Angeles and Yuma, the
conductor came in and began talking to us. . . . 'And so you
are going to Arizona with these two babies? I'm awful sorry.' I
asked him 'Why?,' and he replied, . . . "Only strong men can
endure the heat there . . . [and] the water is not fit to drink in
Arizona. Everybody has to drink whiskey . . ."

Arriving in Florence, she was "charmed . . . by the red
chile hanging in strings . . . mocking birds in wooden cages, boxes
of flowers in the windows . . . It was so new, colorful, and novel
to me." She was to learn that housekeeping had different challenges when all the rooms had dirt floors and that "like all the

INDIAN CHILDREN AT PLAY IN GILA COUNTY,
ARIZONA TERRITORY — AFTER HAVING TO ADAPT TO
AMERICAN CLOTHING, HAIRCUTS, AND SCHOOL.

new comers, I was terribly afraid of everything, especially scorpions and Indians. I don't know which I feared most."

Fortunately, other wives befriended her. She was especially grateful to Pauline Cushman Fryer, the Civil War spy now married to Pinal County Sheriff Jeremiah Fryer. Estella recalled, "Mrs. Fryer . . . told me I must always shake every cloth I picked up, to look all over the bed before retiring for fear of scorpions, to keep the legs of my kitchen cabinet in cans of water on account of ants, . . . and other household knowledge."

Besides watching out for scorpions, concerned mothers also focused on securing an education for their children. Sarah Butler York and her three young children took an 1877 wagon train when they went from Colorado to join her husband in Arizona's Gila Valley, a supposedly six-week trip that took almost three months because of slow oxen and bad weather — "My husband was very proud to think that I would undertake such a journey to be with him, but I told him to make the most of it for, knowing what it meant, I would never do it again, alone."

Mr. York met them in Silver City, New Mexico, where they lived for two years before finally moving to Arizona: "[We lived] for a year in a Jacel house, made by setting posts close together in the ground and daubing them with mud. It had a dirt roof and floor. While we lived at this place, I taught school in one of the rooms, having an enrollment of nine children, including my two. With the proceeds of this venture, I bought my first sewing machine."

After Apaches killed her husband, Sarah and her five children, ranging from age 16 to only eight months, stayed on the Arizona ranch, where the "children's education was a serious problem." She tried sending them to California for schooling, but found the most practical solution was to hire a young lady teacher to live at the ranch.

In 1881, Clara Stillman from Bridgeport, Connecticut, ducked through an opening in a miner's shack, took her place behind her desk — an overturned beer barrel — and began to teach in Bisbee's first school. That first day, as it turned out, was to be a short one. At recess the students discovered a large snake, "coiled and ready to strike," in a corner of the schoolyard. Terrified, but knowing she was on trial with the children, Clara asked them to bring her some rocks and, summoning her courage, battered the snake to death. Then, feeling ill, she dismissed the class.

Not every schoolyard monster was as deadly as a rattlesnake, as teacher Angeline Mitchell (later Angeline M. Brown) remembered: "I was hearing a geography class and feeling something tugging at my dress as if there was a weight on it . . . lying on my dress skirt in a ray of sunlight was as hideous a reptile as I've ever seen. He was black and yellow and tawny and had a body like a monstrous lizard . . . Lord! I gathered up [my] dress and, with a yell one could hear a mile, jumped on the stool . . ."

Her laughing students said, "Why, teacher, that's nothing but a Gila monster." They told her Gila monsters didn't bite unless very angry and that it wasn't easy to make them mad enough, but if you did, they could "blow themselves up."

In all the fuss, the lizard had headed safely down its hole in the corner, but Angie noted later in her diary that the Gila

TWO GIRLS, HAIR CAREFULLY BRAIDED, STROKE A BEARSKIN. A TRAP HANGS ON THE POST TO THE LEFT.

monster came out every morning: "I've taken to picking him gingerly by the tail and putting him back of my desk where he lies out at full length in the sun and sometimes snaps up an unwary fly . . . I stroke his scaly back with a pencil and he likes it apparently. Someday I'll try to make him mad; I want to know if it is true about their "blowing." . . .

In those early years teachers throughout Arizona Territory often had to call on all their resources to meet the challenges of even one short school term. For Clara Stillman, coping with the snake must have made her next hurdle seem easy. Doors, windows, and furniture were luxuries she could forego, but she saw a blackboard as a necessity. With pioneer ingenuity, she improvised by nailing two boards together, painting them, and using a piece of talc as chalk. Another teacher resorted to simply sketching equations and sentences on the sandy floor.

Luckily for Clara Stillman, parents worried that Indians might attack the little shack up a gulch, so they soon relocated classes to the comparative safety of the Miner's Hall in the Brewery Gulch section of Bisbee. Even there, Apache forays made "Indian drills" necessary. Four blasts from the mine whistle — two short, one long, one short — and everyone would troop down into a mine tunnel.

For teachers in rural Tempe, skunks added to the excitement and difficulties. Charles Pickrel, recalling his school days, said that the boys' favorite sport of an evening was to set a trap at an opening under the two-room adobe school building. "The result was invariably a holiday, but never twice by the same teacher," he said.

Schools might be housed in anything from the miner's shack in Bisbee to the saloon in Ehrenberg and the one-time jail in Yuma, where teacher Mary Elizabeth Post reported scribblings of prisoners on the walls still visible through the whitewash. Ingenious improvisations characterized school furniture. Children sat on railroad ties in one school, according to Thamar Richey, and overturned boxes in another. Undaunted by a lack of textbooks, teachers would scavenge the area, even utilizing any books children might bring in from home.

Yet problems of language and class size posed more formidable problems for most teachers than primitive conditions, skunks, or Indian drills. In a preliminary gesture, the Territorial Legislature had mandated schools for communities of sufficient size, but had failed to appropriate any money except for a $250 matching grant offer, which only Prescott seized on to start a school. Augustus Brichta, a Tucson teacher, had to cope with 60 students and was unpaid for two of his six months of teaching at a public school. Not until the 1870s through Governor Safford's determined efforts, did primitive public-funded schools begin to develop in the larger communities.

"A perfect chaos of boys" is how John Spring recalled his experience as the sole teacher in Tucson's first such school. (In 1870, a girls' school was started by nuns, and soon after that, a girls' school was opened by Josephine Brawley Hughes.) By the end of the third day of classes, 138 students had turned up, Spring reported, "not one of whom could express himself intelligently in the English language." Fortunately, he was fluent in Spanish and translated everything he said.

Faced with his enormous enrollment and the language problem, Spring somehow managed to teach for 15 months, but declined the honor of another appointment without an assistant. "He kept them quiet, kept them clean and taught penmanship, arithmetic, drawing, geography and English," according to writer C.L. Sonnichsen.

Parents readily recognized that teachers needed to enforce strict discipline in order to handle their huge and motley classes. In fact, said John Spring, "a great many [parents] seemed to measure the teacher's capacity by his ability to administer severe corporal punishment." Many times, he remembered, parents urged him "to flog a boy to the blood." Once he was asked to beat a youngster who had been sent to buy some coffee for breakfast and had not returned by nightfall, having skipped school as well.

With 18-year-olds in the early grades, it was small wonder that teachers needed to be firm. One of the firmest was George Metcalf, who taught for five years in Tombstone.

"Metcalf had the big kids buffaloed," Charlie Laughlin remembered. "He would pick up the children by the hair of the head and would also pick up boys and bang their heads against the blackboard."

Some male teachers tried valiantly to avoid using corporal punishment. John Rockfellow, Tombstone's teacher in 1890, was noted for being a fine teacher but was thought "too easy" on the children. So was the Reverend Alexander Gilmore, whose class in 1870s Prescott was, in Capt. John Bourke's words, a "miniature bedlam."

According to Bourke, the teacher once tried to punish the worst imp in class, Dick Dana, for throwing a spitball. Young Dick had to wear a dunce cap and stand behind the teacher where the whole class could see him. As Dick meekly obeyed, such quiet fell over the class that Gilmore dozed off. Letting out an exuberant war whoop, Dick grabbed the teacher's toupee, rushed out the door, sprang on his pony, and raced down the street, shouting, "I got ole Gilmore's scalp, and here it is."

AT Q RANCH, MARY ROSE CAMPBELL, DULCIE KYLE, AND GERTRUDE CAMPBELL TEND ONE OF THE LAMBS.

Maria Wakefield, an early Tucson teacher, could no longer control her class when average attendance reached 70.

"You have no discipline," the visiting superintendent told Virgie Robbins when she taught at Crown King. Perhaps he was right, she admitted, recalling that her rebuke to a tiny tot for waving to a passerby met with the response, "That was my Daddy . . . I can wave at him any time if I want to."

Edith Stratton Kitt, later secretary of the Arizona Pioneers Society, found that a show of force could pay off. As a young woman, she taught mining camp youngsters from first to the eighth grade in Helvetia. She once grabbed a girl taller than herself and "shook her so unexpectedly that her head bobbed forward and gave me a bloody nose." But, she added, "all in all we got along fine . . . I never had any trouble with the parents and little with the pupils." Another woman teacher achieved instant authority by hitting the children's hands with a ruler on the first day of class. For teachers still in their teens, using force must have been tempting. Elva Haskell taught in Oak Creek, Red Rock Canyon, Cornville, and Cottonwood in the 1890s. "In all these places I had pupils older than I was," she said.

Creative thinking came to the rescue of some early teachers, notable among them two women who taught on Indian

**A PHOENIX BOY ON HIS BICYCLE WAITS FOR A
PARADE OF FIRE ENGINES TO PASS, CIRCA 1900.**

reservations. Elizabeth White, herself a Hopi, was born and raised near Hotevilla, where she eventually taught. From the start, she decided that she was "not going to let these little children suffer." Her plan was "to take the children on their level of interest from day to day. Never mind about the books." For the first month she helped them learn about objects familiar to them. She also visited their homes. All this time she kept from them the fact that she was a Hopi, so they would be forced to speak English. Under fire for a time for her unorthodox methods, she was eventually recognized as a model teacher.

Gently reared but tough, Minnie Braithwaite from Williamsburg, Virginia, depended entirely on her creative talents when she accepted a job in Navajo country, a position turned down by everyone else because of the inaccessible region and the irascible school head, Mr. Hammer. Minnie had no teaching experience or training, but a sure instinct told her to begin with what was familiar to the children. She started the first day of teaching by having her previously listless students practice writing their own names, and "they were indeed thrilled." From then on, they were her ardent supporters.

Another hurdle Minnie had to vault was Mr. Hammer's insistence that the beginning and advanced students be grouped together. Minnie despaired of teaching with this arrangement until it occurred to her to use the more advanced students to help the beginners.

Mary Elizabeth Post was also up against it when she began to teach at Ehrenberg in 1872. "I had 15 pupils, not one of whom spoke English, and I knew nothing of Spanish." She solved this problem by gathering adults as well as children around her and engaging them in informal conversation as they sat outdoors to escape the heat of the schoolhouse. In this way they learned English and she, Spanish. By autumn when she went to teach in Yuma, she had accumulated a vocabulary of several thousand Spanish words.

For teachers who didn't welcome challenge and dubious adventure, probably the one real advantage of teaching in the early days was job mobility. Male teachers typically stayed on a job only until they had learned enough law to be admitted to law practice, and women were likely to marry after a short teaching stint. But if all they wanted was a change of scene, teachers had no problem finding a new job.

As late as 1880 in Arizona Territory, 102 teachers were responsible for more than 4,000 students. The strain was so great that some schools had to be closed. Given this situation, it's no wonder that anyone who taught for more than two terms in one school was accused of being in a rut.

Even so, an occasional stalwart stayed at his post term after term. M.M. Sherman stuck it out in Tombstone for three years during the heyday of that raw frontier community, 1881 to 1884. "I had to order leaving six-shooters at home," he remembered, "then take their firearms from them [for the day], and finally confiscate [them] till the end of the year."

CHAPTER SEVEN

On the Edge

*Living for the adrenalin rush or just trying
to break the monotony of a day in the mines,
frontier men — and some women —
played their games of chance.*

———◆———

"NO FIRST-CLASS GAMBLER EVER FELT INFERIOR BECAUSE he dealt cards for a livelihood. On the contrary, he often considered himself a superior being," historian C.L. Sonnichsen wrote.

Gambling in the Southwest was usually the most popular male pastime around, especially dominating life in the mining camps. The availability of easy money in a time of speculation was one reason, and it gave an exciting contrast to the drabness of daily life. But the best explanation may be that most of those who ventured West were true gamblers at heart — an optimistic, reckless breed willing to stake everything on an uncertain future. Once there, as old-timer John Cady said of pioneers in the 1860s, "every one of us, each day, gambled his life, so you see the whole of life on the frontier in the early days was one continuous gamble."

Spoken of as a "profession," gambling almost held the same prestige as banking and the law. "It certainly took as much study and a good deal more natural aptitude," commented one observer. Small boys who spent their free time outside gambling houses and saloons took the great gamblers as role models.

Bones Brannon was such a boy in the Tombstone of the 1880s. He fashioned and scavenged the equipment for faro, the "gentlemen's game." A deck of cards, a piece of green cloth, a box with a slot and springs, and he was in business. Bones practiced relentlessly on his friends and his aunt for years, and eventually his toil paid off.

By the time Bones was 21 years old, he was an expert bank dealer. "He could throw the cards out of the box with lightning speed . . . he was cool and deft . . . the intense concentration of the game was a . . . tonic to him." Then after more years of experience in the back-room games, he was ready for the big time. The great Dick Clark let him become a bank dealer at the Alhambra. Another protégé of Clark's was Johnny Bauer, the "Dutch Kid," not educated but handsome, urbane, and possessed of marvelously agile fingers.

Clark was the quintessential big-time gambler, known for his "perfect control." Whatever he might be feeling, he never betrayed fear or appeared rattled. Over 6 feet tall and sporting a Prince Albert coat, "he carried himself like a soldier and spoke with authority." No wonder boys looked up to such a man.

Sleepy Tom Thomas added to the legends of the great gamblers. A dignified man, "his drooping eyelids, flowing tie, and silk topper made him look like a somnolent banker." Domestic troubles he may have had — his wife drove around at all hours in her own horse and buggy and finally ran off with the district attorney — but Sleepy Tom is said simply to have shrugged at the news and returned to the gaming table. His single-minded dedication to his occupation was a characteristic and necessary quality of the successful gamblers.

These determined, clever, cool-headed, and impeccably dressed individuals were often, by all accounts, pillars of their communities. The clergy could always count on the gamblers to come up with sizeable contributions to any worthy cause. The very land on which the University of Arizona stands in Tucson was donated by two gamblers — Ben Parker and E.B. Gifford — and saloon keeper W.S. "Billy" Reed.

When gambling was outlawed in 1907, *The Tombstone Prospector* paid a tribute to the western gambler as distinguished from his eastern counterpart: "The western man assisted in the upbuilding of his country; he reared a family,

**CIGARS, BEER, AND A FRIENDLY GAME OF CARDS
IN PHOENIX, CIRCA 1885.**

contributed to the maintenance of the public schools, encouraged
Christian work, and was often sent to our legislative halls."

Could it be that these pillars of the community were honest as well as generous? A few did have that reputation. Al
Gregg, a faro dealer in early Flagstaff, was reputed to be
strictly honest. It was said that he would refuse to allow anyone to gamble whose losses were too high. Once, when saloon
keeper J.J. Donahue lost $1,000 to Gregg, onlookers reported
that instead of paying, Donahue just "smiled and walked back
to his own saloon." In Tucson, a gambler named Haines kept
his eye on young Mose Drachman when he placed a bet.
Drachman remembered Haines taking him aside later to warn
him against gambling, saying that "the game was honest, but
that the odds were 90 percent against the player and that ultimately I had no chance to win."

The prevailing code of ethics among gamblers was a good
deal more interesting if less straightforward than these stories would seem to indicate. Tin-horn gamblers who used easy
tricks like dealing marked cards were looked on with contempt.

EARLY PROSPECTORS MAYBE WERE GAMBLERS AT HEART, BUT THIS CASUAL PARTY PANS MORE FOR FUN THAN GOLD.

It was only the gambler whose cheating involved a high order of skill who was treated with respect. Such a man for instance, "would not think of holding out an ace or hiding a cold deck under a bandana in his lap . . . but if he had the ability to stack a deck while shuffling or to reverse a cut so smoothly that the other players could not detect the move, he saw nothing un-ethical in employing his hard-earned talent." Besides, skill at cheating, it was pointed out, was the one way of learning how to recognize it in others.

The few women gamblers in Arizona bought into this flexible code of ethics as well. Poker Alice, daughter of an English schoolmaster, prided herself on an honest game but "only the clumsy cheat drew her contempt." She didn't stay in Arizona long, perhaps because of a law prohibiting women from so much as visiting saloons. But the memorable Alice — who refused to gamble on Sunday yet "took her booze straight, smoked cigars . . . and could cuss like a mule skinner" — was not soon forgotten.

Another good-looking, more refined younger woman, about 21 years old, was noted around Tombstone for her modish dress, her diamonds, and her skill as a faro dealer. James

Hancock remembered how she could shuffle a stack of chips. "Many a time I have watched her but she never made a mistake. She was absolutely perfect."

Admirers of these top-notch Western gamblers will appreciate the story involving three New York men who stayed overnight in Tucson on their way to California. Expecting to clean up in what they called this "hick" town's "penny-ante faro games," they started out by tossing down $5,000 for a stack of chips. Bank dealer Ezra Bartlett's response was, "whites are the cheapest I have and a stack will cost you $20,000." With their pride at stake as well as their money, the New Yorkers played — and were "plucked clean" within an hour.

What would a man in Territorial Arizona have done without his saloon? It was the one place he could escape the bleak realities of frontier life. There he could chat with friends, catch up on local happenings, have a drink, conduct a little business, even play cards or indulge in a game of poker or faro. Respectable women, of course, lacked this outlet for company and relaxation, relying instead on religious and social groups.

Described as the "apex of masculine society and the epitome of its culture," the Territorial saloon represented virtually the single solace for men in the early days. Most were unmarried, lonely individuals trying to cope with their primitive surroundings, working long hours in the mines or on a range, and desperate for a little diversion. A mixed blessing for those who drank heavily or lost everything in compulsive gambling, the saloon was a godsend to thousands of others, a place to socialize and forget their troubles for a few hours.

Wherever a few prospectors gathered together, a "saloon" would appear almost overnight. At first it might consist of nothing more than a couple of boards laid across two whisky barrels, but the addition of a tent would turn it into a real saloon. Sam Danner's tent saloon in Tombstone was an outstanding example of such a place. Famous as a gathering spot for gunslingers, it was a large enclosure almost 50 feet square with a dirt floor and light provided by kerosene lamps strung along the ridgepole. A bench stretched the length of the east side of the tent, and here sat an assortment of characters ranging from cow punchers and miners to outlaws.

Devastating fires that destroyed a number of Territorial towns more than once meant that tents, especially tent saloons, continued their useful role beyond the early days. Flagstaff was razed by the great fire of 1886, but within a short time it was "bubbling over with life in the tents, most of which were saloons." When fire burned Morenci, a company mining community, the management decided against leasing any land for saloons. The result? Saloon keepers established another town — Newtown — a mile away consisting of nothing but "saloons and dives with not even a grocery to relieve the sinful monotony."

As towns were built and rebuilt, saloons mushroomed, forming the core of business areas in communities like Prescott, Flagstaff, and Jerome. Nobody ever tried to find a Territorial official in the capitol building, it was said of Prescott during its stint as the Territorial capital. Instead, they would head for the Sazerac saloon. In Phoenix, the Palace was one of the Southwest's greatest saloons. It was "everybody's club house so long as he preserved the peace."

Tombstone alone once boasted 110 places with liquor licenses, many of them saloons. Elaborate structures like the Crystal Palace, the Alhambra, and the Oriental sprang up. A far cry from the old tent saloons, these buildings contained brass and mahogany bars, large mirrors, and oil paintings. Instead of raw whisky or beer, barkeeps in white aprons could mix up "cocktails, mashes sours, cobblers flips, and sangarees." Free food was offered in some places, a welcome addition that may have helped minimize violence.

Piano players and female singers were added, and, at the more pretentious establishments, vaudeville acts. Gambling tales became a common part of the scene offering faro, roulette, monte, poker, and other games. Open 24 hours every day, the

THE SILVER LAKE RESORT, A DANCE HALL AND
GAMBLING ESTABLISHMENT IN TUCSON, CIRCA 1885.

better places were not only clean and expensively decorated
but tried to insist on strict order. Yet, maintaining order was a
continuing problem, especially in the mining communities where
alcohol and gambling made a lethal mix that could end in fights,
even killings. It was no accident that saloons in Jerome and
Pearce were named "Bucket of Blood" and one at Fortuna mine,
"Three Buckets of Blood."

A woman who grew up in the Brewery Gulch area of
Bisbee recalled: "Sure, there was shooting in the saloons at
night. . . . Frequently, it was just a small matter of 'command
performance,' and I do mean command. An innocent bystander
at the bar, perhaps a tenderfoot, guilty of no greater crime than
wearing a coat, vest, and pants to match, a hat and a necktie,
would be commanded by one of the cow punchers, 'Now dance!'
With a six-shooter pointed at your feet, you may not develop
rhythm or a desire to shake a leg, but after a shot or two at
the floor, the 'command' performance began."

It would be hard to exaggerate the amount of liquor tossed
back by the inhabitants of these towns. During Bisbee's heyday,
$75,000 worth of liquor was sold in just one week in neigh-
boring Warren, according to Tom Vaughn, curator of the Bisbee
Mining and Historical Museum.

If drunkenness and violence were much in evidence, an occasional church service in a saloon was not unheard of. Before

Tombstone had any churches, two Methodist barkeeps persuaded the owner of a saloon to close up one Saturday night for
an hour, at which time a prayer service and class were held.
Admission was by ticket only, but the good attendance probably owed something to the free drinks it was known would be
distributed later. A banjo player and singer, Wash Harris, provided lively if unorthodox music for the occasion.

The tone of these establishments was naturally set by
the owners, and these men enjoyed an enviably high status in
Territorial days. Respected as leaders in their communities,
they were often prominent as city officials. Flagstaff saloon
keeper Sandy Donahue served as sheriff of Cococino County
and had a fine reputation as a lawman.

Such men also formed the backbone of many money-
raising efforts. Notable exceptions included John Heath, the
Bisbee barkeeper who planned a robbery and was lynched by
vigilantes irate that he hadn't been condemned to death. Then
there were J.B. Ayers of Charleston and Fred Dodge of
Tombstone, who turned out to be spies for the Wells Fargo
Company.

Much of the life went out of saloons in 1907 with the pro-
hibition of gambling in Arizona Territory. With the state election
of 1914, all saloons had to close their doors.

R anging from the deadly to the ridiculous, formal duels were
still being fought in the Southwest up to the 1890s. More
often than not, the combatants, quick to initiate and accept a
challenge, displayed a curious ambivalence once the match
was on. Shots might go awry, pistols might "misfire," friends
would intervene. One way or another, many antagonists managed to avoid death or even injury.

In an early duel in New Mexico Territory, ex-Major Richard
Weightman, a man known both for his bravery and his temper,
accused Judge Joab Houghton of "conflict of interest, ignorance
of the law" and many other "irregularities." For these provoca-
tive remarks, the judge demanded "the satisfaction due from one

gentleman to another." Weightman was only too eager to accept the challenge.

Their duel with pistols took place near Santa Fe on September 19, 1849. When the command came to fire, Weightman shot, "narrowly" missing Houghton's head, but Houghtman, who may have been deaf, appeared not to hear the command to fire. Weightman then raised both hands in the air and told Houghton to shoot, whereupon the seconds intervened and ended "the ludicrous affair."

In the 1850s, James Tevis, living on a mining claim in southern Arizona, rashly challenged a former neighbor, Tony, who had rudely rejected an invitation to supper by telling Tevis to "go to the devil." Counting on his skill with a six-shooter, Tevis challenged Tony to a duel, only to learn that his opponent, as the challenged party, had the choice of weapons and had opted for bowie knives.

After a sleepless night, Tevis dragged himself to Tony's camp. There, to his enormous relief, he learned that his opponent had undergone a change of heart. Concluding that he had been in the wrong, Tony wanted to drop the whole matter.

"My happiness knew no bounds," Tevis admitted, "and I made a solemn oath never to challenge another man as long as life should last."

In 1859, six-shooters were the weapons of choice. Judge John Watts, Republican candidate for governor of the New Mexico Territory, accused the Democratic candidate, Miguel Otero, of neglecting his duty toward his constituents in the 35th Congress. Otero, he said, had attended a ball with his family while an appropriation bill was pending. Otero's response was couched in such strong language that Watts felt compelled to challenge the other man to a duel.

On the morning of March 7, separated by 15 paces, the duelists took their stand. Each man fired several shots without effect, at which point, "the parties withdrew from the field, the difficulty remaining unsettled." After the event, according to a newspaper account in *The Arizonan*, "Mr. Otero lighted his

TYPICAL HOTHEADED GAMBLER
GOING FOR HIS GUN, CIRCA 1900 —
THE FRONTIER PHOTOGRAPHER
STAGED THIS SHOT AND TREATED IT
TO LOOK LIKE A PAINTING.

cigarillo while Judge Watts amused himself by whistling." All of
which makes it hard to believe that either man seriously planned
to harm the other.

A much less amicable affair erupted between Fred Maish,
a large man and later a mayor of Tucson, and United States
Marshal Milton B. Duffield, also a large man and known as a
violent bully. Maish had repeatedly asked to be paid for a plas-
tering job he had done for Duffield, but which the marshal

had found unsatisfactory. Instead of paying the man, Duffield attacked Maish in a fist fight and then challenged him to a duel.

By this time — 1881— the Howell Code outlawing duels was in effect, so both men were ordered to appear in District Court in October 1881. Duffield was charged with openly initiating a duel. Notorious for carrying concealed weapons, Duffield was told to disarm, whereupon he whipped out two Colt revolvers, leveling them at both judge and sheriff, and announced, "The first man that touches me falls dead."

Quickly, the district attorney stepped behind Duffield, put a derringer to his back, and pulled the trigger, but the weapon misfired. The visibly pale judge postponed the case with a warning to Duffield about carrying weapons. Ultimately. Duffield was heavily fined and put under a $1,000 bond "to keep peace for a year."

In 1880, on the banks of the Blue River near Clifton, a prospector named Hildebrand was camped near a cabin when a deputy sheriff rode up accompanied by a prisoner, known as Markham, on his way to jail.

Hildebrand immediately recognized Markham as the man who had run off with his wife and whom he had been trying to track down for years.

After a verbal exchange, the two men agreed to a duel at five paces. At the count of three both turned, Markham shooting first. Then Hildebrand shot from the hip, and Markham fell to his knees, dead. Hildebrand walked over to Markham's body, fell, and died. On each man's corpse was found a photograph of the same woman.

CHAPTER EIGHT

Making Crime Pay

*A Western audience always enjoyed
a good courtroom drama, but lawyers
certainly made good side shows.*

———◆———

IN THE 1880S, WHEN TOMBSTONE WAS AT ITS WICKED WORST, a lively part of the town's scene was "Rotten Row" located on Fourth Street between Tough Nut and Allen streets. Here a group of low adobe buildings served as offices for as outrageous an assortment of lawyers as ever congregated in Arizona Territory. Four in particular come to mind: Allen English, Ben Goodrich, Marcus Aurelius "Mark" Smith, and William Staehle.

Allen English, tall and handsome with his Van Dyke beard, thick head of hair, and sonorous voice, was the most brilliant of the lot. An East Coast law school graduate at 19, he set his sights on the West, arriving in Tombstone in 1880. Starting with a short stint as a miner, he went on to become a partner of the well-known attorne, Mark Smith. While it soon became apparent that English was addicted to drink, on some occasions, liquor seemed only to sharpen his mind.

Once, while suffering from a hangover, he was obliged to defend gunman Wily Morgen on a murder charge. During the court's lunch recess, he made for a nearby bar where he tossed back a few more and passed out. A friend carried him to the courthouse in a wagon and up the back stairs. It was time for the closing arguments. English rose painfully to his feet and delivered such a powerful speech that the jury was moved to find the defendant innocent on all counts. Yet, according to witnesses, English was still drunk afterward. Typically, he

**1894 PORTRAIT OF THE OFFICERS
AT THE ARIZONA TERRITORIAL PRISON IN YUMA.**

could be "serious, sentimental, indignant, ironic, or poetic as the occasion required." His oratory was larded with Greek and Latin quotations and lines from the English poets. It was said that "the ignorant couldn't keep their mouths closed when Allen opened his."

He delighted the whole town when a judge fined him $25 for contempt of court for being drunk. His rejoinder: "Your Honor, $25 wouldn't pay for half the contempt I have for this court."

His well-earned reputation as a big spender could only add to his reputation in those free-wheeling days. When he

BESIDES KEEPING THE PEACE, TERRITORIAL
SHERIFFS ALSO ASSESSED AND COLLECTED TAXES.
YAVAPAI COUNTY SHERIFF WILLIAM J. MULVENON,
ARIZONA TERRITORY, 1887.

sold his share in the Black Diamond Copper Mine for $84,000, English left for an East Coast shopping spree, buying everything from oil paintings to oriental rugs, all shipped back to his home in Tombstone. Six months later, he returned to Tombstone and paid his tab at King's saloon, leaving himself with only $20 to his name. Divorced by three wives, English lived on into his seventies, "hard up and seedy" at the end, but a legend in his own day.

Mark Smith, who had taken English in as a partner, was himself a legendary figure. A slim, "keen-eyed Kentuckian" with a large mustache, he was eight-time Territorial delegate to Congress and later United States Senator. Smith was both an ardent supporter of statehood and an astute politician. He once admitted to Senator Carl Hayden that he "always tested the political wind at home before taking a stand on Capital Hill," thereby assuring his reelection, even if it made mincemeat of party lines."

If liquor was English's besetting weakness, Smith's was gambling. When friends tried to persuade him to abandon a crooked game at the Pony Saloon, saying he had no chance to win, he offered the immortal response, "What of it, it's the only game in town, ain't it?"

Like English, Smith was an accomplished and witty courtroom lawyer. One summer day when the county attorney had droned on and on until most of the jury was asleep, the sound of a jackass was suddenly heard through the open window. Smith promptly raised an objection. On what grounds, the judge inquired? "I object to two attorneys arguing in court simultaneously," he responded.

A third member of the Rotten Row gang was the colorful William C. Staehle, self-styled "the German Warrior." A hearty little man, Staehle was a gifted violinist with a passion for Mendelsohn. His fondness for liquor soon led his friends to dub him "William Corkscrew." When his flighty wife took off for San Francisco, he was so cheered that he managed to get elected district attorney, an honor that lasted only one term because of his drinking. Like English and Smith, he was loved for his companionability and ready wit. One time he entered the back door of the Crystal Palace Saloon just in time to become embroiled in a fight started by some Fort Huachucua soldiers. Staehle at once held up a finger and yelled, "Count me in." Someone hit him on the ear, knocking him over. On his way down, he again raised a finger and quipped, "Count me out."

A kind man even when he was down and out, he befriended a drunken old woman one evening when she fell flat on her face in front of his door. Carrying her to his own bed, he later dropped in himself in his usual drunken stupor. When he woke up in the morning, there was the old woman next to him — dead. Staehle was terrified lest he be accused of murder, but the coroner's jury did not even mention him, and it was said that "he nearly collapsed under the weight of his own relief."

About as different from his compatriots as one could imagine was Ben Goodrich, fourth member of the Rotten Row crew.

Holbrook, Arizona, *Dec 1st 1899*

Mr. *R B Berryhill*

You are hereby cordially invited to attend the hanging of one

George Smiley, Murderer.

His soul will be swung into eternity on ~~January~~ *Dec* 8, ~~1900~~ *1899*, at 2 o'clock, p. m., sharp.

Latest improved methods in the art of scientific strangulation will be employed and everything possible will be done to make the proceedings cheerful and the execution a success.   **F. J. WATTRON,**
Sheriff of Navajo County.

Revised Statutes of Arizona, Penal Code, Title X., Section 1849, Page 807, makes it obligatory on Sheriff to issue invitations to executions, form (unfortunately) not prescribed.

Holbrook, Arizona, *Jan. 5th* 1900.

Mr. *R B Berryhill*

With feelings of profound sorrow and regret, I hereby invite you to attend and witness the private, decent and humane execution of a human being; name, George Smiley; crime, murder.

The said George Smiley will be ~~executed on~~ January 8, 1900, at 2 o'clock p. m.

You are expected to deport yourself in a respectful manner, and any "flippant" or "unseemly" language or conduct on your part will not be allowed.   Conduct, on anyone's part, bordering on ribaldry and tending to mar the solemnity of the occasion will not be tolerated.

F. J. WATTRON,
Sheriff of Navajo County.

I would suggest that a committee, consisting of Governor Murphy, Editors Dunbar, Randolph and Hull, wait on our next legislature and have a form of invitation to executions embodied in our laws.

NAVAJO COUNTY SHERIFF F.J. WATTRON MADE QUITE A STIR WHEN HE SENT THE FIRST NOTICE FOR GEORGE SMILEY'S HANGING (TOP).

SOME THOUGHT HE WAS TOO FLIP ABOUT SUCH A SOLEMN EVENT.

WATTRON OBLIGED BY SENDING A SECOND INVITATION (BOTTOM).

IN SMALL PRINT, HE SUGGESTS THAT OFFICIALS "EMBED IN OUR LAWS" A PROPER FORM OF NOTICE.

A Texas native, loyal Democrat, and former Confederate lieutenant, Goodrich confounded Tombstone residents by his behavior. He was both a teetotaler and non-gambler — yet he took Mark Smith as a partner in 1881; he didn't frequent the red-light district — but he never attended church. No wonder his eccentric respectability made him an enigma in Tombstone.

"There was everything in Gila City within a few months but a church and a jail, which were accounted barbarisms by the population." So wrote journalist J. Ross Browne in 1863. When the Territory was new, regular jails were almost non-existent. But as the population grew, every kind of criminal began to appear, from horse thieves and murderers to speculators and vagrant politicians. Some action had to be taken, and the Territorial Legislature responded by mandating a jail for every county. For a time, all that this law produced was an assortment of makeshift jails equaled in their variety only by the escapes devised by the prisoners.

"Jail" for offenders in Wickenburg and Globe consisted of tying men to a tree or "snobbing post." In Phoenix, prisoners were chained to a cottonwood log and in Gleason, to a large iron wheel that encircled an oak tree. A variation used in Arivaca consisted of log chains attached to two iron bars buried in a slab of cement. Even more primitive was the jail in Greaterville — a round hole into which miscreants were lowered by rope. Indoor facilities included boxcars in Wilcox and a doorless adobe structure in Pinal County containing a large stone with a metal ring and chain.

An elemental but escape-proof jail was Clifton's "Rock Jail," created from an abandoned mine tunnel in a hillside. This jail contained a large cell for petty offenders and another for dangerous criminals. Floors, walls, and ceilings were all solid rock.

Other jails were equally undesirable. As late as 1890, the Yavapai County jail was described in a letter to the editor of The Champion as "little better than a doghouse." With no ventilation, the cells filled with "foul atmosphere which is liable to produce diseases." Still, by 1880 a second generation of buildings was gradually replacing earlier jails both in Arizona and New Mexico. In the new buildings, the jail was typically in the basement with offices on the first floor and a courtroom, jury rooms, and judge's office on the second floor.

Despite all efforts, escapes continued to be both commonplace and varied. "Jails will not hold their inmates and jurors will not convict," the *Arizona Weekly Citizen* commented about Tombstone in May 1882. The next year, an escaped convict in Globe had the cheek to leave a letter to the sheriff in which he explained that "liberty is sweet to us all, and sometimes laughs at bolts and bars."

Escapes were often managed with the help of an implement smuggled in by friends. In 1895, William Price, sentenced to be hanged, escaped from the Maricopa County jail with the use of two files. These had been pushed through a grated window by a man who, ironically, had reached the high window by way of the scaffolding on an adjacent new jail then under construction.

In 1872 one prisoner feigned illness in order to be allowed outside his cell. Once out, he asked for a drink of water. As soon as the guard's back was turned, the inmate vanished. A newspaper account of the time maintained that even if the first plan hadn't worked, the prisoner would have been freed by friends lurking nearby who were prepared to kill the guard if necessary.

From time to time the human beings behind the labels "prisoner" and "jailor" stand out in some old account. At St. John's jail in 1886 when their tunnel was discovered concealed behind a stack of saddles, the New Mexican prisoners "burst into a real jubilee, laughing and merrymaking." They also told the jailor, John Parks, whom they respected, that they would escape if they ever had a chance, but "Old boy, if we ever get the drop on you, you stand and we won't hurt a hair on your head."

On other occasions it was the jailor who revealed his humanity. As jailor for the Tombstone jail soon after the turn of the century, Joe Axford established an unusual relationship with the 85 inmates. After several jail breaks in which as many as

19 inmates had escaped, Axford was hired on condition that he guarantee an end to the breaks. Discovering that a big problem was boredom from lack of anything to do, he bought boxing gloves, checkers, and a couple of harmonicas. The men borrowed a violin and guitar from friends on the outside, and "before long we had good music on tap," Axford later recalled. Learning of a barber in the group, Axford granted him special privileges in return for doing haircuts and shaves, further improving morale. Most important, Axford made it a point to build a reputation among the men that "my word could be depended on." Because of this trust, prisoners passed on information that helped him foil planned escapes.

The humane jailer at Clifton's Rock Jail returned from a business trip to find flood waters filling the canyon. He plunged at once into the swollen stream on his big horse. Reaching the jail, he leaned from his horse and eventually succeeded in unlocking the door. The prisoners were "hanging to the steel drills in the wall to keep above the water." He rescued them one by one, taking them up to a dry slope.

It was fire that threatened the lives of three inmates in the Flagstaff jail on the night of April 14, 1896. Firemen poured water on the building but could not reach the door so George Hochderffer, the city marshal, and two others frantically chopped an opening in the rear of the jail and saved the inmates.

By the start of the 20th century, iron rings, whipping posts, makeshift jails, and other inadequate structures had generally been replaced by sturdier buildings and better law enforcement. The exploits of the Territorial convicts were passing into history as the Southwest emerged from its riotous adolescence.

CHAPTER NINE

Hotheads, Hermits, and Holy Men

Arizona Territory attracted any number of odd ducks, but there were always enough average citizens around to appreciate the difference.

 ———⟫•⟪———

H ARMLESS OR VIOLENT, EDUCATED OR IGNORANT, ALCO-
holic or sober, Arizona's 19th-century eccentrics were
as diverse and cockeyed a group of humans as you
could hope to meet anywhere.

"Languid, bibulous, ne'er-do-well, and probably the most
cultured man on that frontier," is how someone characterized
Darrel Duppa, one of the Territory's eccentrics who's reputed to
have given Phoenix its name. Born and raised in England,
"Lord" Duppa, as he was called, supposedly had been booted off
to America by his respectable family, anxious to be rid of this
cultivated but wild offspring. Having survived three wounds
from separate Apache attacks, Duppa combined fearlessness
with a knowledge of the classics, a mastery of five languages,
and a penchant for writing poetry.

He chose to live in an isolated stretch of southern Arizona
desert. Capt. John Bourke, an Army officer long associated with
Gen. George Crook and author of the classic memoir *On the
Border With Crook*, thought Duppa's dwelling to be one of the
oddest that he'd seen in Arizona. He described the one-room
ramada as having a roof of branches, unplastered walls, and
an earthen floor. The room was lined with "piles of blankets, rifles, pistols, belts of ammunition, saddles, spurs, and whips."
The Englishman told Bourke that he'd built on that spot because

**IRRIGATING WITH WATER FROM THE SALT RIVER,
FARMERS PLOWED THE DESERT NEAR CAMELBACK MOUNTAIN,
OUTSIDE A TOWN CALLED PHOENIX.**

that was where he'd warded off an Apache attack. Altogether, Bourke found Duppa to be the "queerest specimen of humanity."

Scholarly eccentric Elisha Reavis homesteaded 60 acres in the Superstition Mountains during the 1870s. Called the "Hermit of the Superstitions," he was known for his unvarying costume of seedy coat and overalls, unkempt auburn hair, shaggy eyebrows, and his retinue of burros and dogs. The Indians thought him insane, but Reavis was no fool. Specializing in raising superior vegetables, he was famous for his big parsnips and tender cabbage averaging 10 pounds each. Even among other settlers, Reavis kept an aura of mystery around him by refusing to ever talk about his past life.

Territorial newspapers tended to take a tolerant, almost fond, view of anyone who provided colorful copy, and Algernon Dove certainly did that. Known as "Algy" and "Babe," Dove was familiar to Phoenix citizens, and the papers covered his comings and goings for at least 30 years. A long-time alcoholic, Dove in his earlier days earned respect for taking on hard and dangerous jobs. When a volunteer was needed to carry the mail from the Wickenburg area to the next stop north, Dove was the only one to step forward. He and his horse were shot at on that trip, but he didn't lose his nerve then, or in years to come.

By 1882, though, he was jailed for running around the countryside "bare-headed and bare-footed, reciting . . . fearful

A PHOENIX STREET SCENE, 1872.

accounts and tales, the effects of hallucinations." By 1908, *The Phoenix Gazette* was referring to him as "gentle, tender Algy" with his "insatiable thirst and an unconquerable aversion to work."

The story goes that Dove once entered a Phoenix saloon and announced he was thirsty enough to drink beer out of his boot. Someone offered to pay for all the beers he could drink from that lowly leather container. Dove speedily agreed to the challenge and drank all 17 glasses the bartender poured into his boot. An authority on the dangers of drink, Dove warned against "the danger that lurks in ginger ale," claiming that "it only makes the timid backslider want the real booze more than ever."

A habitué of local jails, he was once asked how he liked Prescott where he had just "wintered."

"The snows there," he reported, "was equaled only by the coldness of the policemen's hearts. What do you think, they even made me go to work! I was stuck with my job a whole day."

Many of the characters of this era were both well bred and well educated. Born to a wealthy Irish family, "Box-Car Riley" earned degrees at the University of Dublin. He suffered a long downhill slide until his embarrassed family shooed him off to America. In Jerome, he worked for a time in the mines and became known for bouts of heavy drinking when he would quote long passages from Shakespeare and the Bible.

Also on the list of educated oddballs from well-to-do families was "Elderberry Bill" who had the habit of gathering elderberries from the mountainside to give to friends. During the time he worked at the Montana Hotel in Jerome, he was laughed at for his custom of dressing for dinner in a formal swallow-tailed coat and striped trousers. These earned him the name of "the Count of no account." His quirks could be traced to a trepanning operation on his skull after a riding accident when he was a young man.

What oddities hard drinking produced in some, lonely desert living encouraged in others. Prospector Ed Schieffelin, whose silver strike gave rise to the town of Tombstone, had prospected with his father and brother since he was a youngster. He'd never known another life and didn't seem to want to. In 1876, before he became famous for Tombstone claim, he was described as having shoulder-length black hair, a long beard, "a tangle of knots," and clothes "so patched with pieces of rabbit skin that he resembled a scrofulous fur-bearing animal." In his single-minded devotion to prospecting, historian John Myers noted, Schieffelin became almost as cut off from the world as a hermit. In his will, he asked "to be buried in the garb of a prospector, my old pick and canteen with me" near the site of his discovery outside of Tombstone.

A different brand of character was notorious for a bad temper, and Bob Winchester was one known for his love of a fight. Once he visited a barber for a shave. A young artist, also present, couldn't resist Winchester's bald pate. While Winchester dozed off in the chair, the artist painted a large tarantula on his head. Upon waking, Winchester made for a restaurant next door, where he doffed his hat, revealing the hideous arachnid to the gaze of a terrified waitress and a group of delighted customers. Winchester furiously hurried back to the barbershop, which he wrecked in short order and was promptly packed off to jail.

During one of his stints in behind bars, Winchester set
fire to his mattress and so added the charge of arson to his
crimes. Next, he made his way to Mexico, but officials there
found him too much to handle and shipped him back.

The frontier gave some men the chance to turn their eccen-
tricities into monumental strengths. Sam Hughes was alleged to have attended school for a total of three days and was
"barely literate," but he became one of the best-known men in
the American Southwest before the Civil War. Historian C.L.
Sonnichsen wrote that Hughes "could do almost anything and
do it successfully."

Hughes was born in Wales and came to the United States
at age eight. By age 11, he was a canal boat boy in Pennsylvania.
Before he turned 21, he had worked as a cotton factory spinner,
blacksmith, and cook. After driving an ox-team to California,
he cooked in a hotel while selling his own pies, canned jellies,
and giant slabs of gingerbread on the side. Next he prospected
gold in Oregon, where he also ran a hotel for a stage line.

At age 29, with an injured back and bad lungs, he moved
to Tucson on a doctor's advice. He soon established himself as
a shrewd and enterprising businessman, buying much property and engaging in mining, ranching, and money lending.
Generally making himself a force to be reckoned with in the
community — he not only helped build up fraternal organiza-
tions, schools, churches, a jail, and courthouse, but also became one of Tucson's mayors — he made no pretense of being
a philanthropist.

"You see," he said, "I owned so much property that I had
to do these things to boost my own game." Few doubted,
though, that his interests in building up Tucson's community
were genuine. "I taught Tucson to toddle," he once said, and "my
hobby was to make a town."

Hughes revealed the same complex personality in acts
requiring courage. When Confederate troops marched into
Tucson and insisted that Hughes take an oath of allegiance or

ESTEVAN OCHOA, ANOTHER DIMUNITIVE TUCSON MAYOR,
WAS THE COURTLY, WELL-EDUCATED SCION OF AN OLD
MEXICAN FAMILY. A HIGHLY PUBLIC-SPIRITED AND
GENEROUS MAN, HE KEPT MUM ABOUT HIS MANY
CHARITABLE DEEDS AND, WITH PARTNER P.R. TULLY,
BECAME ONE OF THE SOUTHWEST'S MERCHANT PRINCES.
BEFORE THE RAILROAD, OCHOA AND TULLY'S
WAGON TRAINS BROUGHT GOODS FROM KANSAS CITY.
CAPT. JOHN BOURKE SAID OCHOA WAS KNOWN AS ONE OF
COOLEST AND BRAVEST MEN IN THE SOUTHWEST.

be shot. Undaunted, the quaint-looking, gnome-like Hughes replied, "I was here before you were, and I won't go."

After further deliberation, however, he did take himself to California until Union troops were again in control.

Preachers fresh from an eastern seminary could be in for a rude shock when they landed in a raw frontier community in the Southwest Territory. In Pinal City, Arizona Territory, in 1881, the new Methodist minister, Reverend Williams, offered a prayer as part of ceremonies dedicating a new schoolhouse. As he stood unobtrusively on the sidelines watching the dance that followed, a "hard-working, good-natured Irish woman, Mrs. O'Boyle," grabbed him by the arm and demanded, "Come on, damn ye! Dont'cha dance?" Chances are, he danced.

Informality was the least of the problems facing the new preacher on the Southwest frontier. He needed to possess mental and physical characteristics radically at odds with the conventional requirements of the position. He often had to endure almost intolerably primitive living conditions and low pay.

"It required lots of bedding to keep from freezing," Rev. Charles Gillett recalled of his early days in Verde Valley when he had to supplement his meager pay from the church by freighting goods from Prescott. Other pastors worked at anything they could get, including mining.

No doubt about it, Territorial preachers had to be physically and mentally tough, like A.J. Benedict, an Amherst College graduate. Benedict had been a member of the Amherst rowing crew that broke the world's record. "Just as handy with his fists as he was with an oar," he was also "the soul of good humor" — no matter how coarse the language in the cow-camps or what the provocation. No wonder the cowboys dubbed him "the cowboy preacher."

Such men needed not only the stamina to endure primitive living conditions, they also had to earn the respect of a diverse population in order to establish churches in the boisterous, secular atmosphere of the time.

Sheer guts and an indestructible sense of humor were two qualities that helped the preacher earn that respect almost as much as physical prowess. In Charleston, near Tombstone, a tall, thin preacher emerged from the stagecoach. He wore black clothes and a high black silk hat. A clutch of local cowboys came to life. Taking careful aim, they riddled his hat with bullet holes. Astonishingly nonchalant, the preacher managed to smile before stepping into a store. He emerged wearing a new hat, this one flat. Walking up to the lounging cowboys, he said affably, "Boys, please don't try it on this hat; my skull reaches to the top, and, besides, I have no money to buy another." Impressed by the man's nerve and good humor, the cowboys became his immediate allies. That same evening they attended his church service and, when a hat was passed, filled it with silver coins.

Reverend Chenowyth lived in Sulphur Springs Valley where he habitually rode his horse several miles to conduct services in a schoolhouse. On one such trip, a young fellow with a gun jumped out from the brush, saying, "Old man, I want that horse."

As Chenowyth obediently dismounted, he told the felon he was on his way to conduct a service and asked whether he might keep his Bible.

"Yes, . . . keep your blankety-blank old Bible; I haven't any use for it."

The preacher casually began loosening some strings behind his saddle, and suddenly the bandit was confronted by a cocked Colt .45. "Now do you want that horse?" Chenowyth asked quietly.

"No, I don't, Daddy. Good-bye," the bandit responded, and vanished into the undergrowth.

Unflappable good humor was an advantage during church services, as well, when interruptions and distractions were commonplace. "Hard work for him to preach," one member of a congregation noted, "on account of dance-hall racket in rear." Other problems included footloose cats, dogs, and drunks, not to mention bawling babies.

The services themselves might be held almost anywhere. In 1880, a Tombstone resident recorded in his diary that he had attended church in tent. Easter Sunday found him at another service — this time in the theater, "a flimsy wooden structure with torn canvas roof."

Baptist parson Bristow preached the first sermon in Verde Valley under a large cottonwood tree. Dance halls, stores, and saloons were also used as places of worship.

To raise the money for a church building, the preacher had to be both enterprising and brash. The most successful men did not hesitate to ask the gambling and business communities to come up with donations.

One Tucson minister always seemed to know when the sheriff and his friends were enjoying a game of poker in a nearby house. The preacher would amble over to watch, and when the jackpot grew large enough, he'd announce, "Boys, I'll take it." No one ever objected.

ST. PAUL'S EPISCOPAL CHURCH IN TOMBSTONE, AS IT LOOKED CIRCA 1884. IT IS NOW ARIZONA'S OLDEST STANDING PROTESTANT CHURCH.

Professional gamblers — who enjoyed an unusually respectable position in those days — and businessmen were often in the forefront of money-raising efforts for churches. Tombstone gamblers, upon learning that Rev. Endicott Peabody lacked money to complete his church, took it upon themselves to make up the difference. At the Silver King Mine, when Methodist minister Reverend Adams asked merchant Perry Wildman for help in locating a building for a church, Wildman strode right into Thompson and Bowen's saloon. There he passed a hat around the gaming tables, collecting a substantial sum. He repeated this effort at two other saloons. Before long, $1200 had been raised, and the church was built using volunteer labor.

In 1895, a popularity contest was held in Jerome between a local saloon keeper and the Catholic priest. Billed as "the wicked against the pure," the contest commanded much local interest. Purity won the most votes, and the priest gave all the winnings to his church.

Unfortunately, frontier conditions that acted as a magnet for preachers of singular mental, physical, and spiritual resources also attracted incompetents and scoundrels.

"It is from politeness to my Maker that I attend church at all here, where numskulls and old broken-down ministers have charge of spirituality," George Parsons complained in his diary in the Tombstone of 1880. No doubt Parsons was outraged by a long, dull sermon, a specialty of the incompetent.

Worse than the dullard or incompetent was the outright crook. It is hardly to be wondered at that a number of bunglers and crooks appeared in the ranks of the clergy during Arizona's wide-open Territorial days. More remarkable is that outstanding men also emerged, men with the unique qualities that the age demanded.

Rev. Endicott Peabody exemplified such men. In his early twenties when he arrived as Tombstone's Episcopal minister in 1882, Reverend Peabody won the respect of the whole community, raised the money for a church, saw it built, and achieved lasting fame as a Tombstone character — all in the space of six months.

One story captures the blend of humor, dedication, and toughness typical of him and others of his caliber. When a parishioner warned that an important contribution to his church came from poker winnings, he thought briefly, grinned, and responded that he had thought of an appropriate adage: "The Lord's pot must be kept boiling, even if it takes the Devil's kindling wood."

CHAPTER TEN

Fine Feathers Don't Always Fly

Between bear attacks, falling boulders,
and Indian raids, clothes could seem trivial,
unless you had the wrong taste in hats.

⟶◦⟵

F OOD, CLOTHING, SHELTER AND WATER — FROM THE PRE-
Territorial 1850s through the early Territorial days,
chances were that the hapless desert or mountain
dweller would find at least one of these basics for survival in
critical or even comical short supply.

Take the matter of clothes. Here is how Daniel Conner,
member of the Walker party traveling in 1862, described the
prospectors and sometime Indian fighters in his group:
"Ragamuffins . . . patched, sewed, strapped and ribboned off
like a Kentucky Bluegrass horseshow in all patterns, fancies,
and designs." If there was no option for vanity in dressing,
there was plenty for both hilarity and suffering as men struggled
to find something — anything it sometimes appeared — with
which to cover themselves.

Comfort and practicality, by all accounts, were the only
rules for men's clothes and footgear. Hence, the man in camp
judged "the most provident and solvent" was the one who had
thought to save cloth flour sacks. These were used for stockings.
With no sewing involved, a man could cut them into a rectan-
gle, fold them around his legs and quickly pull on his boots.

As late as the 1880s, miners in Tombstone wore battered,
stiffened hats, union drawers, and "baggy trousers always ap-
pearing about to fall off." Lem Jett, who hauled lumber in Phoenix

CLOTHES HAD TO BE STURDY, SINCE A MAN MIGHT NOT HAVE OTHERS TO CHANGE INTO.

in the 1880s, prescribed a large hat, thin socks, thick shoes, and no underwear — all in the interests of combating heat.

Clean clothes were scarcely a possibility for men reaching Arizona from the East. George Loring wrote about men in his group who wore once-white overalls now dyed with "blood, bacon grease, smut, dirt, tobacco juice — they look as if they had seen everything but water."

Soldiers in the Southwest dressed little better than civilians, especially when they had been on the move for a time. On the trail of Geronimo in July 1886 near the Yaqui River in southern Arizona, Leonard Wood and his men suffered as temperatures soared to 120 degrees. Marching in heavy uniforms was out of the question; these were soon discarded in favor of drawers and undershirts.

In August, this informal dress almost proved fatal to the group as they neared the Sierra Madre Mountains. When they approached some Mexicans working in the fields, they were mistaken for Indians. "Los Apaches! Los Apaches!" the Mexicans shouted, firing and running for the ranch.

Wood had another close call just after he had persuaded Geronimo to turn himself and his followers over to General Miles. A band of Mexican irregulars approached, bent on taking Geronimo themselves. Wood, dressed in nothing but "a pair of canton flannel drawers, an old blue blouse, moccasins, and a hat without any crown," had trouble convincing the Mexican commander that he was an officer of the United States Army. Finally, the Mexicans halted, but in a very ugly mood.

But shoes and boots posed the most serious threat to an Army man's endurance. Eventually, most traded their poorly made Army boots for moccasins. The crudely constructed boots were made in the Fort Leavenworth prison of "notoriously bad leather." Moccasins, though, were tough and comfortable. Yet even moccasins had their limits. Some of Britton Davis's men found that their moccasins, soaked with water, became useless. They took them off and "for three days had gone barefoot over the sharp rocks and through the cactus-infested slopes of the mountains. Their feet swelled to almost twice their normal size, but they kept up with the scouts by tearing their shirts to pieces and using them for bandages." John Clum also reported that moccasins lasted only about 100 miles, so that every fourth evening became a "resoling party" for him and his Indian allies in their pursuit of Geronimo.

No account of early garb would be complete without mention of the antics of a veteran miner called Smith, a member of the Walker party in 1861. A short, heavyset man who customarily wore buckskins, Smith was unconventional, good-humored, and always ready for a laugh, often at his own expense.

Disliking the feel of wet buckskins against his skin when it rained, Smith took them off one day and buried them to keep them dry. Then he decided to walk downhill almost nude, away

**THESE ARMY MEN — A BUFFALO SOLDIER AND SCOUTS —
ALL WEAR UNIFORM JACKETS AND TROUSERS,
BUT NOTE THE SARTORIAL DIFFERENCE.**

from the cliff where his companions crouched out of the rain. As a game, they rolled rocks down the hill at him. Smith would jump aside only at the last second. Diverted by the approach of a particularly large rock, Smith failed to see a big bear coming. As the animal lunged, the startled Smith let out an "Apache yell" and jumped into the chaparral, while the bear lumbered past. Later, Smith bragged he was "the only man in the party who would . . . receive a bear without having breeches on."

The next day, the men found that they had become infested with "vermin." To rid themselves of these pests, each one stripped and wrapped himself in a blanket. Then they all dipped their clothes into a kettle of boiling water and hung them in the sun. Eventually, the clothes were pronounced dry, and everyone dressed except Smith, who put on all but his buckskins. Slowly, he stooped to pick them up, then let them fall and "they rattled like a dry gourd. His pants being made of buckskin had drawn up to about . . . 18 inches in length and

**ARIZONA WOMEN IN THEIR
SUMMER DRESSES, CIRCA 1900.**

[were] hard as wood." His companions burst into laughter. Smith, with the sure instincts of a clown, leaned over his pants, acting as if afraid to touch them, and, "with one hand resting on his knee for support, walled his eyes up the hill at the merry fellows, without a smile and without a word. This routine brought on another round of laughter."

In the harsh Southwest, nothing was more welcome than a man who could grant a moment of comic relief, like George Hochderffer did. On a Grand Canyon camping trip with his wife and brother in the late 1800s, he found that his wife had mistakenly sewn together two sets of flannel drawers, creating one gigantic pair. Donning the drawers stuffed with pillows, he waddled out to the campfire "on dress parade."

Not all sense of fashion was lost as more women settled the Territory and as trains and wagon teams freighted in more goods of all kinds. Before she married George Brown (later a sheriff and Territorial legislator), young Angeline Mitchell left her Prescott home to teach school in the Tonto district in September 1880. She boarded with one of the ranch families, but even the rough, remote location didn't restrict her wardrobe, as she wrote in her diary describing her attire one hot day:

**STYLISH DOÑA ZENONA MOLINA LEVIN
(MRS. ALEXANDER LEVIN).**

I had on, to be sure, my pet dress for hot after-
noons, a white lawn with delicate pink flowers made
with a ruffle, edges with lace and headed with same
and broad sash of lawn tied at back, tucked waist
trimmed with insertion and lace and a little pink
bow, . . . and rather short ruffled sleeves trimmed with
more of the lace all of ordinary quality and common
style and not new, but clean and crisp, all of my own
make. My stockings were flesh color bal[b]riggan with
pink Indo on the instep . . . My skirts of course were all
white and all trimmed . . . I haven't got a perfectly
plain garment in my wardrobe.

Angie overheard her host tell a visitor, "She looks more
like a living rosebud in that dress than anyone I ever saw, but
she's got grit enough to teach any school around this country."

In 19th-century Arizona, the hat was an object of supreme
importance to soldier and civilian alike — a shield against
sun, rain, rocks, and arrows — but a curious difference in attitude developed between these two groups. The usual rule of

PERSONAL STYLE STILL FOUND EXPRESSION
IN ORNAMENTATION: WHITE MOUNTAIN
APACHES AND THEIR BLACK COMPANION.

strict conformity for the soldier versus freedom of choice for the civilian seemed to reverse itself in the desert.

Army men living outdoors under extreme conditions came to ignore regulations in the interest of survival and a meager measure of comfort. More often than not, officers and enlisted men took whatever hat they were issued and fashioned it to their liking. "Campaign hats were creased, shaped, and dented at the whim of the wearer," one observer noted. Or they wore whatever non-military headgear suited their needs.

An ordinary citizen was more likely to feel the pressure to conform to prevailing frontier styles, which admitedly trended to practicality rather than high fashion.

Even pioneer Albert Banta couldn't ignore local taunts when he rode into Wickenberg wearing a full buckskin suit and a foxskin cap complete with tail.

"Of course," he later admitted, "I was a fool sight to see, but at that time did not realize what an ass I was or how ridiculous I looked."

Foxtail streaming behind him, Banta raced his bronco along Wickenberg's one street as people jeered, "Here he comes, cap and all." Who knew he'd become a newspaper journalist?

More often, it was the unwary newcomer who suffered from taunts. Cowboys loved to scoff at dudes, as Stevenson, a young lawyer, discovered in 1878 upon his arrival in Phoenix. Treated to some snickers when he appeared in a long coat and high hat, he was spared the big treatment until he walked into the Blue Bird Saloon on Saturday night. Encountering a barrage of jeers, he took off his coat and prepared to defend his honor.

Instantly, one joker rammed the hat down onto Stevenson's face; then, someone else grabbed it, and everyone set to work stomping on it. Finally, with what was left of the hat stuck on a pole, the pranksters organized a procession, complete with torches, the Blue Bird's orchestra and vaudeville performer, and a raucous crowd. When they returned to the saloon with the tattered hat, Stevenson took the hint. The next day, he appeared in shirt sleeves and regulation cowboy hat.

Similar treatment awaited newcomers to Tombstone who dared to wear a derby hat on Allen Street. After knocking the offending hat off, locals would take turns kicking it up the street. If the victim kept his temper, the crowd would often buy him an appropriate cowboy hat.

Of course, the Army man understood the importance of comfortable gear, even if the Army did not. "Not a forage cap was to be seen," one writer observed, "not a campaign hat of the style then prescribed by a board of officers . . . Fancy that black enormity of weighty felt, with flapping brim well-nigh a foot in width, absorb the heat of the Arizona sun and concentrating on the cranium of it unhappy wearer!"

As early as the 1850s, the Army had been issuing hats ludicrously unsuited to desert wear. The first of these was the shako or Prince Albert officer's hat, a high, stiff European

THESE FLAGSTAFF LADIES MODEL INTRICATELY TRIMMED FASHIONS — COMPLETE, OF COURSE, WITH HATS.

affair complete with colorful pom-pom. Next came the black felt Jeff Davis hat, which held the heat but lost its shape with the first rain. Also impractical was the dark blue wool forage cap with its high crown that sloped forward and had no reinforcement to hold its shape. Many soldiers turned to broad-brimmed light-colored felt or wool hats, even though not regulation issue.

Relenting somewhat in the 1870s, the Army permitted first the use of straw hats, next a fatigue hat of French design, and finally the *topee*, the cork sun helmet used by English troops in India and Africa. This cork hat, swathed with a light cotton *puggaree*, has been called "the first real concession" made for troops stationed in desert regions.

The Indians were interested observers of the Anglo pre-occupation with hats. They were keenly aware of headgear's

**FORMAL ATTIRE ALWAYS INCLUDED HEADGEAR.
LEFT: NA-BUASH-ITA, APACHE MEDICINE MAN.
RIGHT: WILLIAM BOSHFORD, VOLUNTEER FIRE CHIEF.**

decorative and dramatic uses, and the white man's costume offered new possibilities. At 1884 Fort Grant, 100 scouts used hats as a centerpiece for the feast and dance marking their discharge from the Army. As part of the fun, the scouts "glorified in the most fantastic headgear culled from all the stores on the route": tall black hats, broad-brimmed sailors, even one resembling an old Puritan hat. The celebration lasted far into the next morning.

CHAPTER ELEVEN

Have Fun
or Die Trying

In the face of trying times and uncertain futures,
hard-working Arizonans never gave up on
having a little well-earned fun.

❦

I
N ANGLO SETTLEMENTS, THE ENTIRE COMMUNITY LOOKED forward to races, especially on important holidays. By the Fourth of July 1878, for example, enterprising business-men Allen Stroud and A.W. Mowry were running carriages two miles out to the Phoenix race track every half hour. A crowd of several hundred watched as the winning horses, Black John and Miss Coon Foot, sped across the finish line.

Christmas provided another occasion for races at the Phoenix track. Five horses ran for a purse of $150, according to the December 26, 1878 edition of the *Phoenix Herald*.

In Prescott, horse races up Whisky Row enlivened the Fourth of July and Labor Day festivities. Volunteer fire compa-nies "the Dudes, the Toughs, the O.K.'s and the Hook and Ladder Companies competed in wet and dry tests." (Enthusiasm for all kinds of races in this community generated foot, bicy-cle, and burro races as well.)

In smaller communities, individuals went to great lengths to prepare their own race track. The owners of two horses "would select a stretch of level ground near town and lay out two straight parallel tracks," Jennie Parks Ringgold recalled. Then each man would loosen and remove several inches of soil. Water would be hauled in and poured into the depres-sion, then manure "spread, wet down, and packed." Finally, a

**AFTER A HARD DAY ON THE RANCH, COWPOKES
TOOK THEIR FUN WHERE THEY COULD GET IT.**

layer of soil would be spread on top, with small shoulders left
to hold the water and provide packing.

Star Bay, said to be the fastest horse on the San Pedro,
still lost a race to the scheming of a neighboring rancher. Ben
Snead, stepson of Star Bay's owner, used the champion horse
for roping unbranded calves in winter, but unknown to his step-
father, he made a daily habit of detouring off the OH Ranch
into town, where he spent hours drinking at a Frenchman's establishment. Star Bay grew used to this daily stop and the nose-
bag of rolled barley he got there.

Uncle Billy, owner of a nearby ranch, figured out how to
turn this morning ritual to his advantage. Every so often he
would say in public, "I've got a horse that I think can beat Star
Bay." Ben, a natural-born gambler, heard about this boast and
accepted the challenge.

Since the town's main street was the only straight, level
stretch of land around, it was agreed that the race should take
place there. To no one's surprise, Star Bay took the lead and was
five lengths ahead halfway through the race — until he reached
the Frenchman's establishment, came to a dead stop by his
regular hitching post, and happily awaited his daily allotment
of rolled barley. Uncle Billy's horse galloped past to victory.

JUAN LEVIAS WON THE STEER-ROPING AND BRONC-RIDING EVENTS IN PRESCOTT'S FIRST RODEO IN 1888.

Not only did Ben Snead never live down that race, he was also relieved of his duties as winter cowhand.

Both newspapers and the Territorial Legislature occasionally took exception to some racing. In 1897, the Legislature outlawed racing on the land of one member who was known to lose on races. The *Salt River Herald* confined its attack to the practice of Sunday races on the main street of Phoenix. Labeling them unsafe, harmful to the town's reputation, and an infringement of religious rights to the "blessings" of the Sabbath, the paper pointed out that there was, after all, a race track within three miles of town.

For Indians, the horse race was both an important form of entertainment and a survival technique. The warrior raced his horse frequently and trained him to turn quickly in order to outrun and outmaneuver the enemy.

Horse racing and gambling were the only amusements of the Navajo, S.W. Cozzens noted in his travels in 1858. And Army man C.E.S. Wood observed that "while an Indian is willing to gamble on anything, even a tortoise race, his true delight, the very exultation of his soul, is in a long race between horses of wonderful speed."

Sometimes a serious fight broke out, as in a race in August 1880, as reported by the *Tucson Citizen*. After Juan Elias' colt had won a three-mile race at Junction Station, angry words ensued and eventually led to a full-fledged "cavalry battle,"

**THESE CYCLISTS POSE IN FRONT OF THE MISSION
SAN XAVIER DEL BAC, ARIZONA TERRITORY, CIRCA 1895.**

involving about 40 men. Combatants used spurs to wound each other about the face and body, and after two hours the ground was littered with "torn, trampled and bleeding men."

Races weren't just for horses. People of all ages, conditions, and backgrounds loved foot races in the Territorial Southwest. At the sound of a gun or the drop of a hat, they'd be off — down the street, up a hill, or through the cactus-covered countryside.

The restless energy that brought so many west and the meager options for entertainment kept everyone interested. Placing bets of any amount on a favorite runner also added to its excitement and popularity. In one mining community, spring footraces began with initial bets of $100, culminating by autumn in stakes up to $3,000.

So great was the general interest that some young men trained to be professionals. Such a man was Jesse Pearce who kept himself in top shape through rigorous training. When a horse belonging to Jesse and a friend, Ed Walker, unexpectedly lost a race, Jesse and Ed found themselves in serious financial straits. The solution, they decided, could be a foot race pitting Jesse against a sprinter of local fame, Tom Ortega.

Tom agreed and the race was on. Usually calm, Jesse was so edgy on this occasion that he jumped the gun several times before the race could get under way. But in the event, Tom was no match for the well-trained, highly motivated Jesse, who won by almost 15 feet and recouped his and friend Ed's fortunes.

Fourth of July and other celebrations regularly included foot races. Young men naturally dominated the field, but at a Labor Day picnic in Jerome in the 1890s, everyone got into the act. Prizes were awarded for the young ladies,' the old men's, the fat women's, and the fat men's contests. Children's races were featured in July Fourth races at Joseph City.

Native Americans, accustomed from childhood to running many miles on foot were naturals, particularly for long races. One Indian scout known variously as Cap'n Smylie, Chief Yellow Whiskers and Yellow Face, could run "incredible distances without seeming to tire," according to Army surgeon, Dr. Corbusier. The scout himself remembered that as a young man he often ran 15 to 20 miles with no pause.

The ultimate tribute to Indian foot racers was paid by Geroge Parsons of Tombstone. "These Apaches," he wrote, "are wonderful fast travelers. All they want to know is where you will camp, and they will be there." For Anglos and others the foot race was a welcome diversion or a conditioning exercise. For the Indians it was a part of a way of life.

"Dance crazy" is how one visitor characterized the people of Globe, Arizona, in the 1880s. The description would have fit almost any community in the Southwest territories at the time. Drinking and gambling would remain the pastimes of choice for men, but with the appearance of women, dances came to dominate the social scene.

So popular were they that, if women were in short supply, men would resort to dancing with each other. On one occasion, in an 1860s mining camp, a young man challenged his partner to an endurance dancing contest. Each bet his "coins, coats, hats, boots, and shirts on the outcome," but it was the fiddler who gave out first, and the contestants were spared the ignominy of having to shed their clothes.

**THIS FOURTH OF JULY GATHERING (CIRCA 1882)
WAS TRULY AN ALL-MALE EVENT —
THE "LADY" IN THE MIDDLE IS REALLY A MAN
IN SUN BONNET AND DRESS.
WATERVILLE, NEAR TOMBSTONE.**

Any excuse was enough for a dance, and any place sufficed, whether home, schoolhouse, church, or even outdoors. In Camp Verde, an old-timer remembered that Fourth of July dances, lasting until "after sun-up," were held under the trees with a special platform constructed from logs dragged down the trail by horses. Christmas vied with the Fourth as the most popular time for balls. "They are dancing every night this week," said a Mesa resident in December 1881.

All-night dances were common since the long distances people often traveled to attend encouraged them to stay up once they had arrived. In Flagstaff, dancers would finish up with an outdoor breakfast in the morning sunshine. Families in the hinterland thought nothing of bundling children into the wagon and traveling up to 50 miles for a dance. So determined were the Pomeroys to attend a Thanksgiving ball in Tempe that they traveled in an open carriage in freezing weather, taking with them their two-year-old son.

Helen Wells Heap remembered as a five-year-old in 1876 arriving in a buggy at her grandfather's Chino Valley home for the annual New Year's Day ball. The long living room floor was covered with corn meal to make it slick, a huge fireplace warmed the room, and the "great kitchen" was filled with goodies. She was fascinated both by the dancing and by those merrymakers who, lacking a female companion, would crowd in the corner to tell stories, jokes, and discuss crops and range conditions. After being bedded down in an upstairs room with the other children, she could still hear "the 'Arkansas Traveler,' 'Pop Goes the Weasel,' 'Over the Waves,' and 'Varsovienne,' accompanied by the characteristic scraping, slipping, and sliding sounds of dancing feet below."

For music, people depended on fiddlers, guitarists, and callers capable of drowning out the "whooping and hollering" of the dancers. The Virginia reel, the lancers, the quadrille, and the waltz were popular dances in Tucson that one pioneer remembered.

No dance was complete without the midnight feast. In Walnut Creek, a repast prepared by the ladies might include sandwiches, cake, pies, sometimes oyster stew, and coffee made by the men over an outside fire. At other locations, chicken, ham, and condiments were featured.

Masquerade balls were a great community favorite throughout Arizona Territory. Delighting in the chance for colorful copy, newspapers provided columns-long descriptions of ingenious costumes.

When Jess Hayes was a young man in the early 1900s, his aunt decided he should attend a masquerade in Globe dressed as fiery temperance crusader Carrie Nation. Off he went in a black, lace-trimmed dress, complete with pads on his chest, a wig, black bonnet, and earrings.

Jess wrote later: "The first man who asked me to dance I could not identify. I think he represented a sailor. We started to waltz; neither would talk for we had to hide our identity. Pretty soon he held me a little closer and I twitched my right hand in his left hand. Immediately he held me still closer and I twitched again. The fellow really thought I was a girl who was rather fresh. He asked me for several dances. At unmasking time, he was right in front of me with visions. I took off my mask and he almost fainted. His name was Will Rounday, a good friend of mine. I told the crowd how he acted and he would not speak to me on the street for a long time."

Ever eager for more social life as a boost to morale, the Army carried masquerades to new heights. A rich mix of dances, dinners, and amateur theater took place daily during the 1870s at Fort Whipple near Prescott, but whenever "assembly call" sounded, the men would have to rush from the festive scene and head out on horseback to pursue the Apaches. At a Calico Masquerade at Whipple in 1886, several officers wore pink dominoes and one attended as a rooster with red crest and a long bill. Mrs. George Crook, the general's wife, appeared as Mother Goose.

Although Brigham Young, leader of the Church of Jesus Christ of Latter-day Saints, had inveighed against dancing among the faithful, even the Mormon settlers got into the swing. At Snowflake, Arizona Territory, Jesse Smith lashed out at the practice of "swinging around in a wanton manner" — by which he meant the decadent practice of waltzing — but by the end of the 19th century, criticism had subsided. Church elders looked on tolerantly as young people waltzed away the evening and even took up new steps such as the two-step and fox trot.

Among the general population, grand balls were becoming increasingly popular in places like Flagstaff. Attended by the community's most illustrious, elegantly dressed citizens, these affairs invariably began with a grand march. At last, tiring of this pomp, the Early Hour and Dancing Club of Flagstaff decided on a radical change. To commemorate Washington's birthday, this group threw a "Grand Rag and Picnic Party," complete with gunnysack-and-mattress-ticking attire.

Important as was the social function of dances, they also proved to be the easiest way to raise money for any worthy cause from the Fire Brigade to Ladies' Aid. Veteran railroad builder William Garland even put on a dance to persuade a band of Apaches to grant a right of way through their land for

WITH INDIAN CLUBS ON THE WALL AND BARBELLS AND
FENCING FOILS ON THE FLOOR, THE ATHLETIC MEN OF GLOBE,
ARIZONA TERRITORY, POSE IN THEIR GYM TOGS, 1886.

the Gila Valley, Globe and Northern Railroad. On this occasion
it wasn't only the Indians who enjoyed themselves at the festivities. Chief Engineer Hood was "inveigled into the jollification
and figured quite prominently" as two Apache women took him
in hand and supervised his performance. "Mr. Hood danced,
you bet he did; he cavorted and brought down the house."

In a different category from the social dances
were dance halls and saloons that featured dancing, places
where "respectable" women never ventured. Here, violence
was a fact of life. In Flagstaff, for instance, one proprietor
built a large platform and equipped it with pistols and guns.
"When a valiant gets a little troublesome, he picks him off at a
single shot and that is the end of the creature," commented
one observer.

The threat of violence might hang over even the respectable dance scene in the Southwest. A band of ruffians
came rushing in and pushed to the center of the room in the

middle of a Fourth of July dance put on by Mormons soon after they reached the Gila River. The women each had two revolvers, the men, one each. When someone hid a gun that one man put down, the party crashers created a big ruckus.

In the mining community of La Belle, New Mexico, a group of young men posing as cowboys made themselves part of the town's social life. Not until their later capture did anyone realize that they were part of "Black Jack" Ketchum's outlaw gang.

All in all, the frontier dance scene was a lively one. For a final word on its place in the Territory, turn to faithful diarist George Parsons of Tombstone. On the day that Bisbee gunman John Heath was lynched in Tombstone, a Washington's Birthday ball was also held there. Parson's entry for the day: "Hanging in a.m. and dance in p.m. Good combination."

Not every holiday celebration meant a dance, of course, but in a life where the work never seemed to end, every holiday was good reason to take a rest and have a good time. Some events were solemnly patriotic, others, raucous and goofy.

Prescott, capital of the new Arizona Territory, celebrated its first Fourth of July in 1864. Governor John N. Goodwin reviewed Fort Whipple's troops, and a preacher led the crowd of 500 in prayer. The Army band played the "Star Spangled Banner" and "Battle Cry of the Republic;" the Declaration of Independence was read, in Spanish and English; another Territorial official gave a stirring speech; and a gun salute dramatically concluded the ceremonies.

By 1878, Phoenix was observing the Fourth of July with "races and raffles, picnics and fishing parties, ending up with a grand ball . . . a very brilliant affair — about 60 couples participating." At midnight, an elegant supper was served in two local restaurants.

Patriotic enthusiasm reached an early fever pitch in Mesa on July 3, 1898, when news arrived of a victorious battle in the Spanish-American War — American forces had destroyed the Spanish fleet in Cuba's Santiago Bay. The night sky over Mesa

**A SUNDAY SCHOOL CLASS WAVES AMERICAN FLAGS.
OATMAN, ARIZONA TERRITORY.**

blazed with rockets and Roman candles, accompanied by gun volleys and salutes. The next morning, a spectacular parade gathered with floats of the Goddess of Liberty, Fair Columbia, and Uncle Sam, followed by 200 "little tots" and 80 Rough Riders marching to the rhythms of the Mesa City Band.

Turn-of-the-century Jerome may have opted for fewer pyrotechnics, but still celebrated the Fourth just as vigorously. The slate of activities included sack races, potato races, burro races, bronco-riding and trap-shooting contests, and a scramble for a greased pig, but the highlights were the hose and rock-drilling races.

On holidays and weekends, baseball became a favorite sport in Jerome, whether a man was miner or merchant. The intense rivalry that grew between the Jerome team and the one from neighboring Clarkdale was heightened by a keg of beer always set up behind home plate. The beer could be drunk by those at bat only if they had scored in that inning — or by the other team if they had not. This rivalry eventually climaxed in a brawl that involved even the ladies watching, who engaged in "hat snatching, hair pulling, and name calling."

A simple early Christmas celebration was markedly friendlier. During the Whipple-Beale surveying expedition in 1853, Lieutenant Whipple reported that all took part: Navajo prisoners performed a dance, Mexicans presented a Christmas drama, and the duo of a Crow Indian and a herder sang impromptu ballads telling about the assembled company.

Isolated pine trees were set ablaze for light and warmth, and extra gunpowder was set off just for sheer excitement. The men dipped their tin cups into a kettle of toddy containing rum and wine. Whipple said, "A lively chorus of toasts and jokes ensued, echoing far and wide through the ravines."

Globe owed its first Christmas celebration to a Mr. Jewell. Faced with the problem of finding a large enough space to hold everyone, Jewell settled on the Knox and McNelly saloon. All liquor was removed, and a large symmetrical tree was cut, hauled in, and decorated with ribbons, strings of popcorn, candles, and little mirrors. The merchants gave enough money to assure jackknives for the boys and hair ribbons for the girls. Bags of candy and nuts were distributed, and everyone sang Christmas carols. Some lonely miners rode many miles to be present. The children were ecstatic, and one adult later admitted that he couldn't recall ever having a happier Christmas party.

"Old Bean, the wagon maker, traded four lots to Saxe, the stage driver, for his wife. Had an elegant wedding, married by Marshall, the judge. Everybody got soused and wanted to kiss the bride."

It reads like a spoof, but this account of an 1884 Arizona wedding appeared in the society section of a Casa Grande newspaper. When it came to celebrations, nothing in Arizona Territory was more fun than a wedding.

Pioneer Charles Poston recalled one of the first Anglo weddings in 1850s Arizona before the region became separate from New Mexico Territory. The groom was "handsome young Kentuckian" Sugar Davis. The bride was Anne Aykes, daughter of a well-to-do Tennessean. When he and the wedding guests arrived at the bride's home, Poston said, "[W]e camped on the woodpile and concealed the demi-john of whiskey thereunder."

Anne, for lack of room indoors, was obliged to dress on the back porch in full view of all. Trying to fasten her daughter's

**MR. AND MRS. DEMETRIO AMADO
IN FULL NUPTIAL FINERY.**

corset, Mrs. Aykes put her foot against Anne's body and "threw her weight on the string." Ever helpful, Anne's brother shouted from the woodpile, "That's right, Marm, cinch her 'til she sneezes, and trot her out to be married."

A natural disaster could reduce the ceremony to the essentials, but not necessarily end the celebration. In 1877, groom Bill Duncan had amassed a fortune from the Silver King Mine and planned a gala wedding at Picket Post with his California sweetheart. He imported wines, liquors, and cigars from California, and the women of nearby Florence prepared a feast.

En route, the wedding party was caught by a ferocious June rainstorm. They managed to ford Pinal Creek before it rose too high and took refuge in an abandoned adobe stage station. Soon a large fire blazed in the fireplace, and the company started drinking and singing. Adding to the gaiety was the sight of the drenched bride, a slender blonde whose tight-fitting,

**THIS PATRIOTIC FLOAT, MOUNTED ON A WAGON,
ROLLS THROUGH PRESCOTT ON JULY 4, 1888.**

soaking-wet gown clung to her "like tissue paper bringing out all the fine lines of her shapely form." Her little flowered hat was the worse for the storm — "look[ing] more like last year's bird's nest" — while the groom's face was streaked with black dye from his hat, giving him the look of a "tattooed chief."

A huge pot of coffee was put to boil, bread was baked, and a 20-foot table was laid with ham, bacon, beans, and canned fruit. The merry group at last spread a tarpaulin on the floor and found blankets for the bride and groom. The next day, a rider arrived on horseback with the news that Picket Post, including the wedding site, had been largely destroyed by the flood.

The frontier aura touched even the most carefully planned ceremonies. At the first wedding in a new church in Globe in 1880, the bride, Tonnie Kennedy, moved slowly down the aisle in her "pale-blue silk frock with finger-tip veil." The church was packed, but at the rear stood a man sweating from a long, hard ride. Having no time to remove his spurs — "a serious breach of etiquette," the newspaper sniffed — the disheveled late-comer stood very still in a determined effort to keep from jingling.

Marital arrangements after the wedding were often marked by simplicity and ingenuity, as with those of John Slaughter's Mormon gardener. A bemused surveyor found that a building on Slaughter's ranch — which spread from southeastern Arizona well into Mexico — was actually two buildings connected by a roof but open to east and west. By his calculations, the surveyor could tell that the international boundary between Mexico and the United States passed through the middle of this breezeway. Smiling, Slaughter explained that this enabled his gardener to have two wives without running afoul of U.S. law; one of the wives simply lived in the house in Mexico.

The relief of laughter was an antidote to everyday ills on the frontier, and woe to anyone — civilian or military man — who couldn't take a joke.

Westerners made fun of Easterners when they were handy, of their neighbors when they weren't, and of themselves most often. Life was lonely and isolated enough without letting someone's idiosyncrasies get the better of you. One old-timer showed he'd learned this lesson well when he was asked how he and his business partner managed such an agreeable relationship without keeping written records. "Oh, it has all evened up," he said. "I smoke a pipe, and George wears socks."

Of course, there was always that hilarious incident that didn't seem quite so funny at the time. Frank, a miner living in McCabe, Arizona Territory, around 1899, was wakened early every morning by his neighbor's rooster. This particular morning, Frank hurled his boots at the exasperating bird, but the crowing didn't stop. The furious miner lunged out of bed in his longjohns and chased the rooster back to its owner's cabin, where it escaped Frank's wrath by dodging into the chicken coop.

As he turned to go home, Frank saw an early-morning funeral procession coming down the road. With no other place to hide, he dove into the chicken coop after the rooster. He was

SURVEYORS PICNIC NEAR NEW RIVER IN YAVAPAI COUNTY, ARIZONA TERRITORY, 1892.

forced to crouch, barefoot and shivering, amongst the noisy chickens for most of the morning — even after the procession had passed, two ladies stood in the yard, chatting interminably.

When it came to animal antics, none could match the entertaining cats of Matamoros one celebrated evening. Ordinarily, the town cats could be counted on to keep the rat population under control without fuss.

One night, however, some saloon customers took it into their heads to mix tequila with the cats' milk. Soon the cats were stumbling about. One old yellow tomcat kept on lapping at his saucer until suddenly he raised his wobbling head and squalled. Before the echoes had died, the tom tore across the room at top speed, climbed the wall, and hit the ceiling. He fell to the floor, raced over to the other wall, and repeated the procedure. Finally, he flew down the bar, still squawking, and tipping over the patrons' drinks as he skidded by.

While everyone tried to nab the loco cat on his destructive spin, the other cats drunkenly joined in the chase: "Noise and confusion became so God-awful that the bar was emptied and business was bad for the rest of the night." The tequila-soaked cats continued their feline carouse up and down the streets well into the wee hours.

Amusing stories were simple fun always at hand. Who knows how many chuckled in sympathy telling about poor old George Blank? In Sulphur Springs Valley around 1887, teamsters were hauling lumber from the high Chiricahua Mountains to the mining towns of Bisbee and Tombstone. George Blank supervised the operation.

A likeable man fond of his drink, Blank spent one evening consuming quantities of whiskey. His hangover the next morning had him feeling quite ill, but he still managed to ride his horse along with the rest. As they passed some water flowing from artesian wells, the wretched Blank began to heave once more, but suddenly, his horse also trembled and shook. Fearing he was causing his mount's difficulties, Blank weakly got down, just as a large shock threw him to the ground and into a pool of water. Sure that delirium tremens had finally caught up with him — unaware that an earthquake actually was rocking the entire landscape — Blank cried out, "I've got 'em at last! I've got 'em at last! I'll never take another drink."

In a crude, sometimes cruel, era, the practical joke was regarded by many as the highest form of humor, to be worked on anyone and at any hour. Army scout Al Sieber and friends spent several hours one evening playing pool and drinking in Prescott. Growing hungry, they went in search of supper and passed a butcher shop with large meat hooks hanging from the porch rafters and a drunk stretched out beneath, sound asleep. The temptation was irresistible. The men hung the drunk by his collar on a meat hook, where he swung helplessly until the astonished store owner came to open up the next morning.

Lieutenant Emory, during his stay at John Slaughter's ranch, found a wicked diversion in Viola Slaughter's talking parrot. Irritated by what he thought the banal talk between Mrs. Slaughter and her pet — "Do you love Muzzer?" and "Muzzer's little darling" — Emory decided to take the bird in hand. During Mrs. Slaughter's absence, the officer spent time introducing the bird to some more rough-and-ready expressions. His investment bore fruit when Mrs. Slaughter asked the parrot, "Did Muzzer's little pet have a pretty sleep?" The corrupted bird responded, "Muzzer, you go to Hell, Hell, Hell."

Certain practical jokes were downright diabolical. A young Phoenix lawyer named Kellum dozed off in the pool hall while waiting for his friends to finish their game. Noticing him asleep, Kellum's friends, including Col. C.W. Johnstone, quietly doused the lights, then continued to knock the pool balls together loudly enough to wake him.

Kellum roused and called, "Are you there, Colonel?"

The pranskter cheerily replied, "Was going to wake you as soon as we finished the game."

"Oh, my Gawd," the wretched dupe wailed from the darkness. "I'm blind."

Newcomer Tom Greene reached mile-high Bisbee suffering from altitude-induced fatigue and a buckshot wound. His friends put him on a pool table to sleep while the doctor tended to him. When Greene awoke, Dr. Barney warned, "Don't move suddenly, or you'll bleed to death . . . We had to amputate your leg."

The shocked Greene looked down at his right leg and saw a pile of blood-soaked sheets from the knee down. He groaned in horror, yet insisted that he needed no more anesthetic — his leg just felt numb. No wonder. His friends had tied a cord above the knee of his perfectly whole leg, nearly stopping the circulation. They kept up the pretense for another half hour, finally dragging him off the table while he begged them not to open the end of his "stump."

Not every practical joke had an innovative twist, and the snipe-hunting prank, which is as old as the hills, was a way to relish a new arrival's gullibility. Real marsh birds as snipes are, "snipe hunting" was a thoroughly fraudulent venture. The victim was taken out at night until he was completely lost, then left with a sack and candle and instructions to catch as many snipes as he could get to run into the sack. Sometimes the joke ran its hilarious course until dawn.

Having already fooled a young Jerome newcomer with one of their tricks, two locals decided to introduce him to snipe hunting the hard way. They left the young man, with gunnysack and lantern, at the edge of a marsh. The two scoundrels said they would be setting snipe traps along the trail.

They returned hours later, but found only a hat floating on the marsh water with a torn coat and wrecked lantern nearby. Fearful that the young man had drowned, they hunted for his body in vain, then headed gloomily back to town, where the smiling "victim" awaited them at the local cigar store. Their first prank had left him not quite the tenderfoot they thought him, and to the delight of all present, he'd turned the tables.

Of course, there is more than one way to savor a joke, as journalist George Smalley learned while traveling during the 1880s. One evening on a trail into the Sierra Madres, he came to a little thatched ocotillo cottage. The old Mexican couple inside welcomed him warmly and invited him to spend the night, even offering their own bed. Smalley thanked them, but chose to keep his tarp outside. He watched as the old lady laboriously worked to build up a fire for cooking a pot of beans.

As he waited, Smalley asked the woman about some red berries growing on a nearby bush.

"Eat some, and you will see," she told him in Spanish.

Smalley thrust a handful of berries into his mouth, a surrender to curiousity that he instantly regretted. Rushing to the well, he spat out the berries and gulped cold water to assuage "the fire that was raging in my mouth and throat. The old lady and her husband laughed heartily. It was a good joke on their Gringo guest and my first introduction to chili tepina."

PHOTOGRAPH CREDITS:

COVER: Farmer, Arizona Dept. of Library, Archives & Public Records (ADLAPR), Archives Div.; family, ADLAPR, Archives Div., #98-1604; execution notice, Arizona Historical Society/Tucson; cowboy with baby, ADLAPR, Archives Div., #98-0414; lantern, Sharlot Hall Museum; wagon, Sharlot Hall Museum, #PO-160P; father and son, Arizona Historical Society/Tucson, #46490; Chiricahua Apaches, ADLAPR, Archives Div., #98-6070; buffalo soldier, Arizona Historical Society/Tucson, #B109357.

CHAPTER FIVE
Page 62   Yuma County Historical Society, #3286.
Page 65   Arizona Historical Society/Tucson, #4893.

CHAPTER SIX
Page 68   Arizona Historical Society/Tucson, #46490.
Page 70   Prescott Sharlot Hall Museum, #PO-693P.
Page 72   Arizona Historical Society/Tucson, #377.
Page 74   ADLAPR, Archives Division, Phoenix, #99-0097.
Page 76   Arizona Historical Society/Tucson, #22782.
Page 79   Arizona Historical Society/Tucson, #22856.
Page 80   ADLAPR, Archives Division, Phoenix, #96-4427.

CHAPTER SEVEN
Page 84   ADLAPR, Archives Division, Phoenix, #98-0452.
Page 85   Prescott Sharlot Hall Museum, #M-101P.
Page 88   ADLAPR, Archives Division, Phoenix, #97-0748.
Page 91   ADLAPR, Archives Division, Phoenix, #97-4665.

CHAPTER EIGHT
Page 94   File.
Page 95   Arizona Historical Society/Tucson, #60613.
Page 97   Arizona Historical Society/Tucson.

CHAPTER NINE
Page 102 ADLAPR, Archives Division, Phoenix.
Page 103 ADLAPR, Archives Division, Phoenix, #97-7182D.
Page 106 Prescott Sharlot Hall Museum, #PO-2087P.
Page 109 Arizona Historical Society/Tucson, #5189.

CHAPTER TEN
Page 112 Arizona Historical Society/Tucson, #2017.
Page 114 Arizona Historical Society/Tucson, #B109357, #B113018, #B113022.
Page 115 ADLAPR, Archives Division, Phoenix, #99-0107.
Page 116 Arizona Historical Society/Tucson, #40908.
Page 117 Arizona Historical Society/Tucson, #50140.
Page 119 Cline Library, Special Collections and Archives and Public Records,
          Northern Arizona University, #NAU.PH.660-97, 109735A.
Page 120 Na-buash-ita. Arizona Historical Society/Tucson, #17774. William
          Boshford. Prescott Sharlot Hall Museum, #PO-911PA.

CHAPTER ELEVEN
Page 122 Arizona Historical Society/Tucson, #49695.
Page 123 Prescott Sharlot Hall Museum.
Page 124 Arizona Historical Society/Tucson, #B68674.
Page 126 Arizona Historical Society/Tucson, #8289.
Page 129 Arizona Historical Society/Tucson, #61145.
Page 131 Arizona Historical Society/Tucson, #2215.
Page 133 Arizona Historical Society/Tucson, #57399.
Page 134 Prescott Sharlot Hall Museum.
Page 136 Arizona Historical Society/Tucson, #8087.

VOLUME 10

DOUBLE CROSS
Treachery in the Apache Wars

Fear . . . hatred . . . killing . . . revenge

This terrible cycle antagonized settler-Apache relations on the Arizona frontier. Double-crossing set the stage until the Apache Wars were inevitable, and treachery remained an ugly and driving force during years of war. Depending on your point of view, devious maneuverings on all sides either contributed to the settling of the Southwest or further subjugated native peoples, but no side — career officers, Apache leaders, Mexican troops, ranchers — had a copyright on treachery.

In 13 chapters, history author Leo W. Banks resurrects specific betrayals from a dark and bloody past. Some of the earliest were crucial in shaping the future of Apache-Anglo relations.

A scalp-hunter, during an 1837 trading session, turns a cannon on an Apache chief and his band. Geronimo breaks his promise to surrender in Canyon de los Embudos in 1885 . . . Mexican irregulars, supposed allies in the fight against the Apaches, murder Capt. Emmet Crawford . . . an Apache defects and guides American troops to a stunning success in Mexico . . . Gen. George Crook faces bitter political betrayal by his successor, General Nelson Miles.

Read these stories and others of the old-fashioned double-cross in a book that lets you smell the camp coffee, hear the bugle and the war cry, and see the men fall in the cruel canyons of the Apache Wars. Do the ends justify the means? Readers can be the judge.

Softcover. 144 pages. Black and white historical photographs.
#ABTP2 $7.95
Coming in October 2001
Ordering Information on Page 144

WILD WEST COLLECTION

VOLUME 1

DAYS OF DESTINY
Fate Beckons Desperados & Lawmen

Many came West intent on molding a future, but every chain of events has a single day, a fleeting moment, when fate points a decisive finger and the flow of history changes. Here unfold 20 tales of how real-life desperados and lawmen faced days that changed their lives forever.

Softcover. 144 pages. Black and white illustrations and historical photographs. **#ADAP6 $7.95**

VOLUME 2

MANHUNTS & MASSACRES

Clever ambushes, horrific massacres, and dogged pursuits — each true story catapults the reader into days of savagery, suspense, and conflict in Arizona Territory. If life was hard, death came even harder.

Softcover. 144 pages. Black and white historical photographs. **#AMMP7 $7.95**

VOLUME 3

THEY LEFT THEIR MARK
Heroes and Rogues of Arizona History

Indians, scouts, and adventurers of all sorts gallop through 16 true stories of individualists who left their unique stamp — good or bad — on Arizona's early days.

Softcover. 144 pages. Black and white historical photographs. **#ATMP7 $7.95**

VOLUME 4

THE LAW OF THE GUN

Recounting the colorful lives of gunfighters, lawmen, and outlaws, historian Marshall Trimble explores the mystique of the Old West and how guns played into that fascination.

Softcover. 192 pages. Black and white historical photographs. **#AGNP7 $8.95**

WILD WEST COLLECTION

VOLUME 5
TOMBSTONE CHRONICLES
Tough Folks, Wild Times

When Ed Schieffelin struck silver, thousands flocked to a rough Arizona mining camp, transforming Tombstone into an oasis of decadence, culture, and reckless violence. Here are 17 true stories from a town where anything could happen — and too often did.

Softcover. 144 pages. Black and white historical photographs. **#AWTP8** $7.95

VOLUME 6
STALWART WOMEN
Frontier Stories of Indomitable Spirit

Tough enough to walk barefoot through miles of desert. Strong enough to fell a man with a jaw-crunching blow. For danger and adventure, read these 15 riveting portraits of gutsy women in the Old West.

Softcover. 144 pages. Black and white historical photographs. **#AWWP8** $7.95

VOLUME 7
INTO THE UNKNOWN
Adventure on the Spanish Colonial Frontier

Centuries before Wyatt Earp and Billy the Kid, Spanish-speaking pioneers and gunslingers roamed regions including what now is the American West. Going where no non-Indian had gone before, they lived and died in a wild new world, lured — even driven — by the power of the unknown.

Softcover. 144 pages. Illustrated. **#ASCS9** $7.95

VOLUME 8
RATTLESNAKE BLUES
Dispatches From a Snakebit Territory

Here are the stories you've never heard. Funny. Outrageous. Ridiculous. True accounts of the news, yarns, and utter lies about Arizona Territory that ran in newspapers of the day.

Softcover. 144 pages. Black and white historical photographs. **#ATHP0** $7.95

TO ORDER THESE BOOKS OR TO REQUEST A CATALOG, CONTACT:
Arizona Highways, 2039 West Lewis Avenue, Phoenix, AZ 85009-2893.
Or send a fax to 602-254-4505. Or call toll-free nationwide 1-800-543-5432.
(In the Phoenix area or outside the U.S., call 602-712-2000.)
Visit us at www.arizonahighways.com to order online.